SOCCER GOALIE

OTHER BOOKS BY LES ETTER

MORNING GLORY QUARTERBACK

BULL PEN HERO

Bobbs-Merrill Co.

GOLDEN GLOVES CHALLENGER

BIG DOWN GAMBLE

Hastings House

SOCCER GOALIE

BY LES ETTER

Illustrated by Francis Chauncy

HASTINGS HOUSE, PUBLISHERS

New York

To Paul Etter
U.S. Marine

A BRIEF INTRODUCTION
TO SOCCER

Soccer is truly a world-wide game. Historians tell us that a form of it was played as far back as 2,500 years ago in China. The Romans are supposed to have introduced it to Great Britain where it became extremely popular during medieval times, gradually evolving into the game we know today. It spread to all parts of the world to become a major sport everywhere except the United States. In this country it has been far overshadowed by American football, baseball and basketball until recently.

There are reportedly 185,000,000 registered soccer players in the world at present but few of them know it as soccer; to them the game is football, as it is called in Olympic Games competition. The word soccer itself is an abbreviation or nickname taken from the game's correct title, Association Football.

It is almost impossible to estimate the millions of

people in the world who watch the game in person or on television, particularly in England, Europe and South America. Soccer also is popular throughout Asia and Africa.

Every four years most nations in the world compete for the World Cup, a slender statuette that has become what is perhaps the most coveted sports trophy in the world. By a series of eliminations, 14 countries will qualify for the next Cup series in Mexico in 1970.

More than 1,500,000 people watched the last series, and the final game between England and West Germany was seen on live television by an estimated 400 million in the biggest world hook-up in TV history up to that time. It also was estimated that during this time half a billion fans followed the matches through newspapers, radio and TV. In England alone some two million fans pack the stadiums every Saturday afternoon from September through May. The same can be said for the parks of Rio de Janeiro, Paris, Barcelona, Madrid, Moscow, Prague, or even Bangkok. How much more international can one get?

Few people ever heard of an ex-Brazilian bootblack named Edson Arantes do Nascimento, but mention King Pele of the Santos team of Brazil on the streets of any major city on the globe, and sport fans will know instantly who you mean. Even in the United States his name has become a familiar one in recent years.

There are other names such as Bobby Charlton of England, Denis Law of Scotland, Best of Northern Ireland, or Eusebio of Portugal—to mention just a few who are recognized everywhere as great names in soccer.

Professionally, the emergence of the North American Soccer League, a coast-to-coast network of 17 teams in the

United States and Canada, with resulting TV exposure, is a giant step toward making the sport more popular in this country. The league followed the merging in 1968 of the National Professional Soccer League and the United States Soccer Association.

While practically all of the players come from other countries, the growth of the sport should lead to the development of great players of American birth and the eventual development of a United States team to compete for the World Cup.

Growth of the game also is on the upswing in colleges, universities, preparatory and high schools throughout the country. More than 500 college teams are playing, and this number is increasing rapidly. There are literally thousands of teams at prep and high school levels, not to mention park league play.

The National Collegiate Athletic Association has had championship competition since 1959, and there are a number of well-established college and university conferences such as the Ivy League, New England, Middle Atlantic and Rocky Mountain loops. These are only a few of the leagues that come to mind.

Perhaps ignorance has been the sport's greatest handicap in the United States. Although football, baseball and basketball still hold the spotlight, there is a growing awareness of the advantages of soccer. It is an invigorating and colorful game, and it costs little to equip a team. The game also provides real participation opportunities for athletic boys who lack the bulk and brawn necessary for American football.

THE EQUIPMENT—Players wear shirts, shorts, stockings, shin guards and special shoes. Soccer shoes have cleats of leather, rubber, nylon or light alloys. Any item that might cause injury to another player has been removed.

THE BALL—The ball must be spherical and have an outer casing of an approved material, usually leather. It must be 27 to 28 inches in circumference and weigh between 14 and 16 ounces at the start of a game.

THE FIELD—Overall dimensions of the playing field range from 100 yards (minimum) to 130 yards (maximum) in length, and from 50 to 100 yards in width. To conform with international standards the average field is 110–120 yards long by 70–80 wide. The sides are marked by touchlines. These are joined at the ends of the field by goal lines. Corner flags (5 ft. high) help to determine whether the ball has gone out of play.

A center line running the width of the field divides it into equal halves. At the middle of it is the spot where the game starts, and re-starts after a goal is scored. A circle of 10 yards radius is marked around this spot. This is called the center circle to ensure application of one of soccer's most common laws—that opposing players must be at least 10 yards from the ball whenever a dead ball situation occurs, as on the kickoff, free kicks, goal kicks or corner kicks.

THE PENALTY AREA—This area is 44 yards wide by 18 yards deep. Any of the game's nine penal offenses committed within its limits by a defending player awards a penalty shot to an opposing player from the penalty spot 12 yards in front of the goal. It also indicates the area in which a goalkeeper is allowed to touch the ball without being penalized.

THE GOAL AREA—This area is within the penalty area and measures 20 yards wide by 6 deep. It serves two purposes: (1) when a goal kick is being taken, the ball must be placed within the goal area, (2) when the goalkeeper has the ball, or is obstructing an opponent, he can be charged—otherwise he has special protection within the goal area.

THE GOAL—The object of the game is quite elementary—to get the ball into the opponent's goal, an area 24 feet wide by 8 feet high, marked by two uprights joined by a crossbar at the top. Nets may be attached to the framework to contain the ball after a goal has been scored.

TEAM BY POSITIONS—A soccer team consists of 11 players. There is a goalkeeper, two fullbacks, three halfbacks, five forwards.

The fullbacks are designated as right and left fullbacks, and often known as "the backs." There are three halfbacks—right half, center half and left half. The forwards include outside and inside right forwards; center forward, and inside left and outside left forwards. The outside men also are known as wings.

It is imperative that the opposing teams wear different colored uniforms. The goalkeepers also wear uniforms to distinguish them from the rest of their team and from other players on the field since they are the only players permitted to play the ball with their hands. This is for identification purposes by the referee.

Because soccer is such a fast, fluid game with the action moving swiftly from one end of the field to the other, there is no time for the type of signals prevalent in American football. However, the game calls for a high degree of team-work, and success depends upon the players being in the right place at the right time. They must be constantly alert to shift from offense to defense immediately.

The five forwards comprise the line that usually swarms down the field to try for a goal. They are the best dribblers on the team and the best pass receivers. They take the corner kicks, pick up clearing kicks from their own goalies and fullbacks.

The halfbacks are two-way players. They are considered the first line of defense as well as the men who back up the offense, often starting plays. They work with the wingmen usually on offense and the fullbacks on defense.

Fullbacks are the last line of defense with the goalie. They must always keep between the man with the ball and the goal, without backing into or blocking the goaltender. They must be good volley kickers and excellent headers. (Players are allowed to use their heads to push the ball where they want it to go.)

Compared to the other players, the goalie has little running to do. But he must be agile, alert, courageous and cool. He must be able to use his hands, feet and body to block the ball and know instantly when to come out and dive on it. A goalie can throw the ball with one hand, and he must be able to catch it or deflect it away from the net.

SOCCER RULES—Soccer is an easy game to understand. There are few rules—17 in all—established both to control the game and to protect the players.

THE GAME—is divided into two equal parts—45 minutes in each half. At the end of 90 minutes of play, the team with the most goals is the winner. In NCAA competition, however, four 22-minute quarters are played, and in case of a tie, two 5-minute extra periods are played. The usual intermission between halves is 10 minutes.

SCORING—A goal is scored when the whole of the ball legally passes over the goal line between the goal posts and under the crossbar.

START OF THE GAME—The kickoff is made from the center spot at midfield. (All players must be in their own half of the field.) After a goal is scored, the game is re-started in the same manner.

THROW-IN—When the ball is played over the side-line, a Throw In is taken by any player of the opposing team. (The ball must be thrown from behind the head, with the player facing the field with both feet on the ground.)

CORNER KICK—When the ball has been played over the end line by the defensive team, a Corner Kick is awarded to the team on offense, the kick to be taken by any player from within the quarter circle at the corner of the field.

GOAL KICK—When a player of the team on offense plays the ball over the end line a Goal Kick is awarded to the defensive team. The kick is usually taken by the goalkeeper, but may be taken by any player from within the goal area. The ball is not in play until it has passed outside the penalty area.

REFEREE DROPPING BALL—If play is stopped by the referee while the ball is in play for any reason other than an infraction, the game is re-started by the referee dropping the ball between two players, one from each team. The ball must touch the ground before it can be played.

OFFSIDE—A player on offense is offside when there

are less than two opponents closer to their goal line than the player receiving the ball *at the time the ball* is passed to him. (Note that the goalie counts as a player.) A player cannot be offside if he receives the ball from an opponent, from a goal kick, a corner kick, a throw in or from a referee drop ball.

FOULS AND MISCONDUCT—Bodily contact does occur in soccer . . . and plenty of it but to deliberately play the man instead of the ball is in complete violation of the rules.

FREE KICKS—Awarded as a result of fouls. Fouls must be evidently intentional.

DIRECT FREE KICK—Awarded at spot of foul for tripping, kicking, holding, striking, pushing, charging violently, charging an opponent from behind, jumping at an opponent, handling the ball. The kick may be taken by any player. A goal may be scored direct.

PENALTY KICK—For any of the foregoing offenses committed by a player in his own penalty area, a penalty kick is awarded. The kick may be taken by any player from the penalty spot, which is 12 yards directly in front of the goal. Only the defending goalie may face it.

INDIRECT FREE KICK—Technical or minor fouls call for an indirect free kick. The difference in this case is that a goal *may not* be scored from the kick unless the ball touches another player enroute. Such fouls include: (1) The goalkeeper taking more than four steps without releasing the ball. (2) Dangerous play. (3) Ungentlemanly conduct. (4) Intentional obstruction.

• • • • • 1 • • • • •

JOHNNY PARKER turned quickly from the dormitory window and kicked his luggage violently against the wall. Of
all the things he could do without, a view overlooking the
football practice field a block away was all of them rolled
into one.

A single glimpse of the tiny figures working out there
was like a physical blow. It brought back all of the frustration he had steeled himself against during the summer,
knowing that big-time college football was not for him—
not for a guy standing only five-eight, and weighing one
hundred fifty pounds.

Besides, Midwestern had a great quarterback in Slade
Carson, and he finally realized he was no competition for
the rangy passing star. In one sense it was a relief—he no
longer had to listen to Carson's stinging remarks about his
small size, and the other wisecracks Slade directed at him.

So he was back at college again as a sophomore pre-medic student, wrapped in gloomy thoughts, wondering what his new roommate would be like.

There was a quick knock on the door and a black-thatched youth wearing a sport jacket entered the room, smiling at him.

"You must be Parker," the stranger said easily. "I'm Vic Lockridge—engineering. Looks like we're stuck with each other." He thrust forth his hand. "For better or for worse," he grinned.

Johnny got up. "Right—Johnny Parker. Glad to know you."

Lockridge studied him quizzically. "Say, aren't you the Parker who got hurt in spring football—knee or something?"

"Collarbone," corrected Johnny shortly, trying not to wince. "That's me, all right—old Brittle Bones Parker."

"Sorry," apologized Lockridge. "That explains why you're not out at practice." He smiled sympathetically. "I know how you feel. When I was sixteen I broke my leg skiing, and it kept me out of soccer for a whole year. Man —I thought my little world had ended right there!"

Johnny Parker looked at his roommate with new interest. He liked this cleancut-looking guy with the healthy tan and the friendly manner. But a shadow crossed his face. "I'm afraid I'll miss more than one season. I'm through with football—period. Too many bigger and better men available—especially Slade Carson. I was tackling him when I got hurt."

"Oh, I say! I'm really sorry. How about other sports?"

"What other sports?" Johnny asked bitterly. Then he quickly changed the subject, not wanting to offend his new friend. "You say you play soccer?" he inquired politely. "Where?"

"I started in Toronto, Canada, where I was born. Then I played at a boarding school in the French Alps. My dad was overseas manager for a plastics company. I played a bit in England, too, while I stayed with Mother there. So when I entered Midwestern I turned out for the team here."

"The team here?" Johnny asked blankly. He knew that soccer was not a varsity sport, and then remembered that there was some sort of student club on the campus.

Soccer had never greatly interested him. There had been no soccer in his home town of Bloomfield except as a part of his grade-school gym classes. He also had played a little during summer recreation camp. As far as he was concerned it was strictly a fun game like tennis or volleyball; though he knew it was a major sport in Europe and South America because he had read about the riots at the big games there.

Lockridge smiled. "I know it doesn't rate with American football or basketball," he said. "But really, it's quite a sport, you know—requires more skill than most people imagine—more than I have, certainly, but I love it. Ever play?"

"Just gym class or summer camp." Johnny's voice trailed off. "Football is—or was—my game. I don't know much about soccer."

"That's a pity," Vic said, and then his face lit up eagerly. "You know if we make a good showing here this season, the athletic board has promised to consider making soccer a varsity sport. A lot of colleges play it on an intercollegiate level, and the game is growing in this country all the time. If we go varsity we can get a good schedule and travel more. Right now we pretty much finance ourselves."

"I hope you make it," replied Johnny. "I know they have a NCAA championship in soccer."

"Indeed they do!" said Lockridge. "We hope to play in that kind of competition before long. Thanks for the good wishes, old man!"

As they unpacked, Vic continued to discuss his favorite game. To Johnny's surprise he found himself catching some of his roommate's enthusiasm.

"Soccer probably is the oldest organized sport in the world," Vic explained. "The Chinese played it twenty-five hundred years ago. The winning team got wined and dined by the emperor while the captain of the losing team got flogged publicly."

"Man! What an incentive!" exclaimed Johnny.

"Right! There are lots of interesting things in soccer history. The Romans are supposed to have brought it to Great Britain. Through the centuries it got so popular it threatened to supplant archery as the national pastime, and the nobles tried to stop it. It also got so rough that King Edward III banned it in 1365—and got nowhere. The people simply ignored the royal decree and went on playing. But I don't want to bore you with a lot of ancient history."

Vic reached into his bag and pulled out what appeared to be a worn pair of low-cut football shoes. "Ever see a pair of these before?" he asked. "A lot like yours, aren't they?"

"They certainly are."

"Our game is different, though, as you know—much more running, no ball handling except by the goalkeeper or on throw-ins. Even in a tackle you play the ball and not the man. Soccer really puts the foot in football."

Johnny inspected the shoes critically. "Looks like you wear almost the same size I do, even if you are bigger."

"I'm taller, of course, at six-one, but at one-sixty-five pounds, I probably don't weigh too much more than you. That's another thing about soccer—you don't have to weigh a ton to play. Size may help, of course, but a good little man can make a monkey out of a bigger man every time if he has skill. Some of the greatest players have been small men—especially wingers."

Seeing that Johnny was still examining the shoes, Vic said, "Why not try 'em on? I've some new ones—just kept these in case of emergency."

"What are you trying to do? Sell me?" Johnny's smile was good-humored. He was pleased at Lockridge's interest; he was beginning to feel as if he had known Vic for a long time.

"That might not be the worst idea you ever had," replied Vic Lockridge seriously. "You might like it. We don't get big crowds or much glory here at Midwestern, but we do have fun. Besides, you are an athlete—you should do something physical. Sound mind in a sound body, you know."

Johnny frowned. The past was too recent. "Me—play soccer? I'm afraid not. I'd be a real square. Maybe I'll polish up my golf. Who knows but what I may be another Jack Nicklaus? He was a collegian, you know—Ohio State."

"Well, who knows but what you might be a great natural soccer player? You'll never know unless you try. We could use more manpower on our squad. We never have over twenty-five men, hardly enough to scrimmage. There are a few exchange students from England, one from Germany, and another from Brazil. They've all played quite a bit. The rest of us are sandlotters, or former prep or high school players. We do have a fine coach, though. Mac Henson was a pro in England and Canada, and he coached a bit before he came here to join the physical education staff. He's doing some teaching, and coaching us on the side. We're hoping he can continue as our coach if soccer reaches a collegiate level here."

"Maybe you've got a point," Johnny said thoughtfully. "But I don't want to strike out again."

Vic looked at him quickly. "You don't impress me as the sort of chap who would worry about that."

"What do you mean?"

"No harm intended," replied Lockridge. "Anyway, it's your own affair."

Johnny felt a touch of bitterness again—would he ever be able to forget football? Maybe this was the time to find out.

They finished unpacking in silence, and then Lockridge asked, "What time do you get up in the morning? Do you have a first hour?"

"Yeah, I'm stuck," replied Johnny. "I get up at seven." Then he asked, "What time did you say soccer practice started?"

Vic's face widened in a smile. "I didn't," he said, "but we start at four—behind old Watterson gym. Think you can make it?"

"I'll give it a whirl, but don't look for a miracle."

"Why not meet me at three-thirty?" asked Lockridge eagerly. "I can show you the ropes and introduce you to Mac Henson." He stood up and started for the door. "I'm heading for the bookstore," he announced. "I'll get us a soccer rule book. And by the way—don't forget to give me a shake in the morning before you leave. I often oversleep, you know." Vic Lockridge went out whistling softly.

Johnny smiled after him; he was going to like this guy very much. The smile faded as he thought about soccer, and then he shrugged.

What did he have to lose?

····· **2** ·····

JOHNNY was impressed by Mac Henson. The soccer coach was a stocky man in his late thirties, with thinning brown hair receding from a peak above a ruddy, square-jawed face. A dented nose made him look more like an ex-boxer than a former soccer star.

Henson's handshake was firm, his smile friendly, but his keen brown eyes were steady and appraising. He did not look like the sort of man who would beat around the bush.

"Glad to have you with us, Parker," he said. "Vic phoned me about you. We need good men but you'll find soccer much different than American football. I hope you find it interesting. I'm sure you can learn the game, but condition is the big thing now. Without wind and good legs, a soccer player is nothing. It's run, run, run—and then run some more. That plus kicking and ball control.

Fundamentals can be taught. Stamina is something you build up day by day through the hardest kind of work. There are no shortcuts. How does that sound to you?"

"I'll try to give it all I've got."

"Good! Now then—" Henson pointed to Johnny's feet. "Those shoes are too big—too loose. A couple of days of practice and you won't even be walking, for the blisters."

Johnny explained about the borrowed shoes, but the coach shook his head. "Unless you wear snug-fitting shoes, you are beaten before you start. This is a game of feet, you know."

The rest of his equipment, also loaned by Lockridge, proved to be adequate—a light jersey, trunks, stockings, and shin-guards.

As Lockridge mentioned, the squad was small, about twenty-five players in all, and of these, several did not look like athletes to Johnny. He could not help but contrast this group with the nearly one hundred hand-picked candidates at a major football squad turnout.

Practice began with the squad running several laps around the inside perimeter of the field. In this respect, soccer was no different than American football, Johnny thought. Next, several soccer balls were tossed out and the players began kicking easily to each other, or dribbling with their feet. Later they practiced heading, or meeting the ball with their foreheads, passing it with a quick thrust of the neck muscles.

Johnny felt awkward and self-conscious as he tried to learn these fundamentals. He had to force himself not to catch the ball with his hands, as he would have done in almost any other type of sport.

He watched Lockridge trap the ball with his body

and let it fall at his feet in a kicking position. He tried to emulate Vic but his reflexes betrayed him as he caught the leather in both hands.

Instantly Henson shouted, "That's a foul, Parker. That means a free kick for your opponent in a game. Let's do it right!"

"Learn to kick with either foot," advised Lockridge. "Almost anyone can kick with the right foot. Try the left— keep working at it until you can use either one naturally."

The squad also practiced volleying, or kicking the ball before it touched the ground. Some of the players were quite skillful at this, and at trapping high kicks with their bodies.

Johnny had difficulty dribbling the ball, or advancing it with a series of short kicks, or taps as they are called in soccer.

"Keep your eye on it," Henson said. "Don't kick with your toe. Use you instep, and keep your ankles loose. You must acquire a touch for the ball, and don't let it get too far ahead of you, or you'll lose control."

Heading the ball, or propelling it with the forehead, also was something new for Johnny. It took timing and strong neck muscles to meet a swiftly propelled object 28 inches in diameter, weighing approximately one pound, with the forehead and aim it accurately in another direction.

"It's a matter of proper timing," Henson cautioned. "Don't let the ball hit you. Meet it first. Take it about hairline level on either side of the forehead—like this." The coach sent a high pass lofting easily toward Lockridge. "See what I mean? It's not hard—just takes practice."

The session wore on. Johnny's leg muscles grew heavy, and the last few minutes were sheer torture. He sighed with relief when the coach blew his whistle. But his sigh was cut short.

"Everybody take four laps around the field!" ordered Henson. "No corner cutting! Let's go!"

Johnny groaned. Where had he heard that before? American football and soccer had another thing in common. He began plodding with the others around the endless confines of old Watterson.

As they left the field, Lockridge introduced him to some of the other candidates. Red Watson, Vic's running mate at fullback, was a tall, muscular fellow with closely-cropped auburn hair.

"Red is from New York," explained Vic. "A great high school player there, and he's a good man to have on your side in a clutch."

Then he indicated a dark-haired, dark-skinned athlete with a flashing smile. He could not have been more than five feet, five inches tall, and Johnny estimated his weight at one hundred thirty-five pounds.

"Tony Cardenas, our left winger," Vic said. "Brazil's gift to our team. He's living proof that a little man can excel in this game."

Both players greeted him cordially. Johnny was particularly interested in Cardenas. He had marked him as the fastest man on the team during the workout.

When they reached the dressing room, Johnny groaned again. "Wow! Will I be stiff tomorrow! I didn't know I had so many muscles! Football is a pipe compared to this!"

"Join the party," Watson said with a grin. "We'll all be aching. I've played football, too, so I know what you mean."

Only Cardenas seemed still fresh and smiling. "I run all the time," he explained. "Besides I do not have the weight you carry. Back in Santiago, I even tried the marathon once." He made a face. "Too monotonous. I like soccer better."

As the group showered and changed to street clothes, Johnny met more members of the squad. There was Ron Beatty, a ruddy-cheeked, flaxen-haired British exchange student who played left halfback—there were three halfbacks in soccer, Johnny already knew.

Vic introduced Andy Bronfeld from Milwaukee, the center half; Bob Thompson, the inside right forward, tall and strongly-made, from New Jersey, and Rick Weaver, a stocky youth of medium height, with heavy eyebrows and a rather sullen expression. His home was in Chicago, Vic said.

All but Weaver greeted him warmly. As they left him, Vic said carelessly, "Don't mind Rick. He's a moody chap —rather aloof, you might say. But he's one heck of a center forward. Just takes getting used to."

Next to Cardenas, Johnny was most impressed by Ernst Kessler, a blond giant from West Germany with a mop of shaggy sun-bleached hair.

"Ernst is as good as any college goalkeeper around," said Lockridge. "He could play on any amateur team."

Keller bobbed his head in a formal little bow. "That Victor," he smiled. "Always saying nice things." Then he added, "I watched you today. You have been in athletics before. You will learn soccer quickly."

They were a nice gang, Johnny thought, as he finished dressing. Even Weaver probably was okay. It had been a lucky break, having Vic Lockridge for a roommate.

Next morning as they breakfasted together in the dormitory dining room, Vic said to Johnny, "I have that rule book. Soccer rules, of course, are completely different than you are used to. A bit of brushing up wouldn't hurt me either. If you like, we could quizz each other for a few minutes each evening."

Realizing how little he knew about the game, Johnny eagerly agreed. There were eleven men on a side, he had learned, the same as in football. A team consisted of a goalkeeper, a pair of fullbacks, three halfbacks and a five-man forward line. The front line carried the brunt of the offense. It consisted of a center forward, right and left inside forwards, and two wingers, corresponding somewhat to ends in football.

The goalie and the fullbacks were basically defensemen while the halfbacks—center, right and left—served as sort of backbone for the team, supporting the defensive and also backing up the offensive forward line.

The object of the game, he knew, was to move the ball toward the opponents' goal by use of the feet, head and body until a goal was scored. It was a much more fluid game than football since the teams shifted from offense to defense with great rapidity. Ball control, field vision and ability to seize the initiative instantly were most important.

As a former T-formation quarterback, Johnny wondered about offensive formations and plays. These he soon learned were actually more like basketball and hockey than

American football. Vic told him that good strategy meant getting a man free for a try at the goal. The defense seemed basically to be man-to-man although there were variations.

As they studied the rulebook, Vic emphasized to Johnny that since Henson wanted his team in collegiate competition next year, they would play under NCAA regulations this season.

"Basically the rules are the same as the international laws," he said, "except that colleges play four twenty-two minute quarters, while the pros play two forty-five minute halves. College teams also are allowed more subs in the game, and ties may be played off in two five minute periods."

Lockridge continued. "Our field is one hundred twenty yards long by seventy-five wide. International standards can be both longer and wider, although most of them are close to NCAA dimensions."

"Brother, our field seems larger than that," said Johnny. "I've never run so much in my life!"

"You are used to American football. A gridiron is only a hundred yards long and about two-thirds as wide as a soccer field." Vic grinned. "Besides football is easier. You stand around a lot."

"Ever get tackled by a two hundred pound linebacker?"

"If he tackled that way in soccer he could get thrown out of the game. The least he'd do would be to give up a penalty shot."

"At least I know that," replied Johnny. "In soccer, tackling is a means of getting the ball away from an opponent—with your feet. You can't put your hands on him."

"Correct! Please remember that."

Thoroughly sold on soccer now, Johnny bought shoes of the proper size; he could sell them if things did not work out.

During the warm-up next day, Henson tapped a ball toward him and pointed to Cardenas twenty yards away. "Pass it to Tony," he ordered.

Johnny thrust his right toe against the leather and it sailed ten feet above the Brazilian's head.

"All muscle, no control!" snorted the coach. "Use the instep, man! The inside of your foot! When you put a shoe to a soccer ball you must know exactly where it's going! Try again!"

Gradually he learned the various types of kicks and how to control them. Henson taught him to use his left foot, and his passing improved. "Watch Weaver and Cardenas," advised the coach. "You can learn a lot from them. Ask questions, too."

Johnny hesitated to approach Rick Weaver but Cardenas seemed delighted to help him. "How long did it take you to learn to dribble like that?" he asked Tony, as he watched him tap the ball from side to side in front of him as he ran, dodged and feinted.

"Ever since I was little I have played soccer," replied Cardenas. "In Brazil kids play soccer just like baseball here. In the U.S., it is Micky Mantle. In Brazil, it is King Pele, the greatest soccer player of all time! There is nothing he cannot do with a ball! Did you know he is the highest paid athlete in the world?"

The little Brazilian showed him how to trap the ball

with his feet, legs or body, how to volley, or kick the ball while it is in the air, how to head it and how to pass it backward with the heel.

"You have the speed," complimented Tony. "With experience you could be a halfback, or even a wing."

Henson was less optimistic. "The name of this game is ball control," he warned. "Until you can put that old balloon exactly where you want it, you're just another body out there. And watch those hands—I see you still want to use them."

Sometimes Johnny envied husky Ernst Kessler. At least the goalkeeper could catch and throw a ball as well as kick it. Ernst often came out from the goal to smother shots with a dive, or punch it away with his fist. He could spring up quickly after a dive to kick or throw the ball far down the field or else roll it softly to a nearby mate. Sometimes he shouted helpful advice to the defense. He would have made a fine football linebacker, Johnny thought.

Once after Kessler uncoiled like a giant spring to block a high corner shot, Cardenas shook his head in admiration. "If anything happens to our Ernst, we are in deep trouble," he said.

As practice progressed, Johnny usually played as an inside halfback on the second team in daily scrimmage. His quarterback experience had taught him to analyze strong points of both offensive and defensive gridiron play. Now he turned this talent to soccer.

He learned that Andy Bronfeld at center half, was one of the most important cogs on the team. Andy dictated field tactics like a quarterback although his primary job was to cover the center forward on the opposing team since this post usually was filled by the best scorer. He would have little chance of replacing Bronfeld.

Weaver at center forward was probably the squad's most gifted all-around player. He was an excellent shot and a fine passer, although not quite as fast as Cardenas. But like Tony he could dribble at top speed, and he could give any goalkeeper real problems.

One day Johnny's football habit of using his hands almost proved disastrous. Weaver broke up the middle, eluded Bronfeld and headed for the goal, dribbling swiftly. Johnny wheeled across the field to cut him off but he was a step behind.

Instinctively he hit Rick with a regular football tackle, and Weaver crashed to the turf, the ball bounding off to one side.

The whistle shrilled, and Henson grabbed Johnny by the shoulder. "Get off the field!" shouted the coach. "That was the most flagrant foul I've ever seen!"

Weaver lay limp while Henson and Lockridge worked to revive him. Finally he was helped to the bench where he sat groggily holding an icepack to his head.

After Johnny had listened to some more of Henson's blistering comments, he looked anxiously toward Rick and hurried up to him.

"I'm sorry, Rick," he apologized. "That was a heck of a thing to do, but I guess I just forgot myself."

Weaver glared at him. "Oh yeah? Forget the apology! If that's the way you want it, that's all right with me! Just remember two can play this game! I've heard about you before—"

Henson broke in angrily on their conversation. "Par-

ker, I told you to go get dressed," he snapped. "Then wait around—I want to talk to you after practice. Weaver, let's have none of that kind of talk! I'm satisfied it was an accident, even though we just can't have that kind of stuff. So forget it!"

The coach abruptly turned back to practice as Johnny headed for the dressing room. As he changed clothes he felt angry and disgusted with himself. Would he ever learn how to play this silly game? Another thought struck his mind as he thought of Weaver's last words. What had he meant? What had he heard before? But there was no use trying to talk to Rick at this time.

Henson spoke more calmly after the others had left the dressing room following practice.

"I can understand how it happened," the coach said, "but the point is we can't tolerate that kind of play. Weaver could have been seriously injured by a tackle like that. In football, players are padded and braced to take that kind of punishment. In soccer they are not. I know the change from one kind of game to another must be difficult, but you've got to face it. We all realize you didn't mean it—or you wouldn't be here now."

Johnny cleared his throat. "I'm sorry, sir. I certainly won't let it happen again. But what about Weaver? He seems to think I meant it—"

Henson waved the thought aside. "Forget about Rick! Naturally he was upset. He'll feel differently by tomorrow morning. If he doesn't, I'll set him straight. Now let's start off tomorrow with a clean slate—see you then."

Although Henson's words made Johnny feel better, he still wondered what Weaver had meant by his last crack.

He mentioned the incident to Lockridge back in their room.

Vic frowned thoughtfully for several moments. "Didn't you tell me one day that you and Slade Carson didn't see eye-to-eye in football? Wasn't he the guy you tackled when you got that broken collarbone?"

Johnny stared at his roommate in surprise. "Yeah, that's right, but what's that got to do with what happened today?"

"Maybe nothing," replied Vic. "Except that Carson and Weaver are fraternity brothers."

····· 3 ·····

ERNST KESSLER was about to be late for soccer practice. His chemistry experiment had taken longer than he had expected, so he hurried from the science building to his motorcycle in the adjacent parking lot.

Kessler was an expert motorcyclist but now he was in a hurry. He roared out into traffic, just made it past a changing light and was side-swiped by a swerving truck. He skidded across the curb and fell heavily on the sidewalk as an excruciating pain shot through his right leg.

While he was being hoisted into an ambulance a little later, Johnny Parker and Vic Lockridge on their way to practice, joined the curious crowd of bystanders.

"It's Ernst!" gasped Vic just as the ambulance door closed.

Johnny turned to a policeman seeking information from the truck driver.

"We're friends of the fellow who got hurt," he said. "How bad was it?"

"Looked like a broken leg," replied the officer, "but you better check with the hospital. They'll have the correct dope."

They thanked the officer and left to seek Mac Henson. The coach acted swiftly. After calling the hospital to learn that Ernst had a compound fracture, Henson quickly outlined the extent of the goalie's injuries to the squad.

"Kessler is out for the season, there's no doubt about that," he said soberly. "I guess you all know what that means to us. Since none of you has ever played goalkeeper before, I'm asking for volunteers. It will take somebody with plenty of courage and agility, and above all—good hands."

Good hands! In the dismal silence that greeted the coach's remarks, Johnny Parker had an inspiration. Good hands, Henson had said. Well, what was he waiting for? He might have a chance to play first string. He certainly could not make it as a halfback or winger now.

"I'd like to try it," he said as he cleared his throat self-consciously. He could feel the eyes of the others upon him, and he expected someone to laugh. When no one did, he chuckled himself to cover his embarrassment. "I guess everybody here knows I use my hands, all right. I'm not much good any place else—maybe I'm a natural goal-keeper."

Henson looked at him sharply. "You are serious, Parker? This is certainly no time for humor."

"I'm not trying to be funny," protested Johnny. "I've played football where use of the hands is essential, especially at quarterback. I can throw and catch a ball. Goal-keeper is one spot where I can use what skills I have."

Henson's eyes lighted. "I believe you have a point," he said. "There's no harm in trying you. We've got to have someone."

While the other players loosened up, the coach sent Johnny into the goalie's position. "I'll fire a few at you, and we'll see how you react."

A soccer goal is twenty-four feet across the front and eight feet high. Nets are attached to it, stretching back to a depth of two feet. It seemed like a tremendous area to protect, Johnny thought, much larger than it looked when he had rushed at it on attack.

Henson placed the ball on the penalty mark twelve yards from the center of the goal as Johnny stared at him in dismay. He had hardly expected the coach to try the most difficult of all shots to block as a starting test.

"All set?" asked Henson.

"Okay." Johnny crouched tensely, his eyes on the ball.

Mac Henson did not try to fool him. Instead he drove the leather straight at him like a bullet. He barely had time to see it start curving to the left as he leaped out to block it. His hands flew up instinctively. The hurtling sphere drove through them to rebound from his chest. He flung himself after it in a smothering dive. He clutched it to his body and came to his feet.

Henson's expression did not change as he took the re-turn toss. This time he came forward, tapping the ball in a slow dribble. Suddenly it whizzed off his left instep. Johnny waved at it futilely as it spun into the net just below the crossbar.

"When you get a high one like that, punch it away or tip it over the bar!" snapped the coach. "You can't possibly get in front of it!"

Henson drilled shots at him from every angle as Johnny grew desperate. A few he blocked, some he even deflected. Two or three times he managed to make a diving lunge out in front of the goal to retrieve the ball. Here his football fundamentals helped—he had practiced falling on the ball often enough.

Finally Henson waved him aside and Johnny's heart sank. As he was about to turn away, the coach said briefly, "Get you breath. You'll take over goalkeeper in scrimmage today."

During the next half hour the first team seemed to take personal pleasure in driving blistering shots past him. Weaver, in particular, came at him with blazing speed. Twice he blocked cannonball drives, but Rick's third shot almost drove through the net.

"Keep your eyes on the ball, Parker!" stormed Henson. "You should have had that one!"

But Johnny did not draw all the coach's wrath as he shouted at the fullbacks. "Watson! Lockridge! Wake up! The goalie can't do it all alone. What are you out there for?"

When the session was over, Johnny felt exhausted and let down, but Henson said, "Not bad for a start. We'll try you again tomorrow."

As he stayed in the goalkeepers post, Johnny began to gain confidence. He found he could analyze the attack patterns flowing toward him and position himself accordingly.

"Anticipation is half of it," Henson said. "That, and never losing sight of the ball."

He received a crash course in the art of goalkeeping. Henson was with him every moment he could spare. He showed his protégé how to handle high and low shots, and tricky bounders, demonstrated how to smother shots and clear them. There were corner kicks to be dealt with, and also free kicks and penalty shots. Johnny practiced goal kicks so that he could spell the fullbacks, and Henson showed him how to tip shots back over the crossbar.

The coach seemed impressed with his jumping ability. "For a little chap, you certainly take to the air. Where did you learn to jump like that?"

"Believe it or not," Johnny grinned, "in high school I was a high jumper. We didn't have any tall kids who were any good. I wasn't either but I was all we had, just good enough to get a letter."

"Amazing," said Henson. "Well, it's paying off now. Not many men your height can go so high. Of course, there have been good short goalies, but all things being equal, a tall man has a better chance. After all the underside of the bar is eight feet above the ground."

Johnny smiled to himself. It gave him satisfaction to know that there was one phase of this game in which he did not have to yield to taller men.

The squad members who at first had seemed neutral about his progress, began to regain their confidence. Even though they realized he was no Ernst Kessler, their comments were encouraging rather than skeptical.

One afternoon after he had blocked several difficult shots, even turning back Weaver and Cardenas, he felt elated as he entered the dressing room after the workout. But he sank down on the bench tired from the strain of the last few minutes during which Henson had been stressing attack.

Lockridge slapped him on the shoulder. "That's the best you've looked out there, Johnny," he said. "You're beginning to act like an old pro."

Even though he felt this was flattery it sounded good, and when Cardenas, too, spoke to him, he felt even more grateful.

"I thought the coach was spoiling a halfback to make a poor goalkeeper," said Cardenas. "But Henson is smarter than I am. He's making a goalie out of you—maybe a real good one."

Weaver passed, heading for the shower. "What do you mean, Tony?" he asked. "Why, Parker was really carrying a horseshoe today! I had him beaten twice, and what happened? The ball hit the crossbar. He never even saw it! He couldn't even tie Kessler's boots!"

The room became silent as Johnny stood up quickly. "I'll grant you that I'm no Kessler," he said. "But don't try to alibi your lousy shooting by using me. If you want to cry, go home and sulk on Carson's shoulder. You're two of a kind."

Weaver whirled around. "You can't talk to me that way!" he said, his face white with anger. But as he stepped forward Lockridge and Bronfeld moved in quickly.

"Knock it off!" Vic said sharply. "Quit acting like a couple of grammar school kids. If Henson hears this, both of you are in trouble."

Rick Weaver sneered. "What can he do? We're only a

club. Anybody can walk out of here who wants to. Nobody's paying my tuition here."

"Nobody here is getting his tuition paid for playing soccer," said Bronfeld. "That goes for all of us. But I think we all should have enough loyalty to stick together. If anybody doesn't like it that way, then it's time to get out."

"Meaning what?" snarled Weaver.

"For the last time, cut it out and cool off," snapped Lockridge. "Let's all forget it now. We'll feel better in the morning."

Weaver was silent for a moment, then his eyes swept around the room. "Guess I'm out of order," he said sullenly. "I'm sorry, but some things get my goat."

Johnny turned away and tossed his shoes into the locker. He remained silent, but some things also got his goat.

4

MAC HENSON was not in the locker room during the encounter between Johnny and Weaver, and it was just as well. He had enough worries of his own.

Foremost in his mind at the moment was the weakness at goalie. Although Parker was showing progress, it was not coming fast enough. It looked as if the Bobcats would go into their ten-game schedule with an untried rookie in goal. The boy had potential ability, but the opening match with the Ohio Tech Hornets was just a week away.

His second problem was the Midwestern athletic board. Sometimes he wondered why he bothered with soccer at all. He had a salaried position on the staff, not a big paying one to be sure, but when he received his doctorate there would be more money as well. However, he loved the sport—it had been his life since he could remember—

and he was determined to pioneer it at Midwestern to the intercollegiate level where it belonged. Mac Henson was a dedicated man—and this could be the best team he had ever had at the Bobcat institution—if only this one player could come through.

As he sat in his cubbyhole office in dusty old Watterson gym, Mac surveyed his situation. Crowds at games last season had been meager, to say the least. The attendance had to be boosted this year to satisfy the board that the sport was worth its salt. But how? It would take a miracle to get many students out to watch soccer when their native interests were centered around football and basketball. Henson was certain, however, that once they had been exposed to the game, they would become interested.

As an old professional player he realized the value of publicity, of some gimmick that would attract a crowd. If he could get one good idea, perhaps he could enlist the student paper, the Midwestern *Chronicle,* to start the ball rolling.

Henson leaned back in his swivel chair and stared out of the window where a gym class was booting a soccer ball around with abandon and great lack of skill. Then his eyes narrowed and he leaned forward; he had an angle that just might work.

Seizing the telephone on his desk, he dialed the number of the *Chronicle,* then asked for the sports editor. He realized the young editor personally covered football and wrote a daily column, but this was soccer and Henson was at his dedicated best at this moment.

"I've got a real feature for you," he said brightly after he had identified himself. "I'm sure you'll like it."

"Yeah?" the sports editor sounded suspicious and

slightly bored. Then he apparently realized he was talking to a faculty member. "I mean yessir," he said cautiously. "Could you tell me what it's all about?" It was the first time the soccer coach had ever called him with anything except a match score.

"You remember Johnny Parker, the quarterback who was injured in football last spring?" asked Henson. "Well, he's our first string goalkeeper now since Ernst Kessler, our regular goalie broke his leg. I'm sure you could get an interesting story out of a comparison between the two sports by a fellow who has played both of them. Soccer is a growing sport in this country, you know."

The editor's voice still sounded dubious. "Well, it might be okay, but right now we're short of reporters—"

Henson did not give up easily and finally the *Chronicle* man agreed rather grudgingly to send a reporter out to practice next day. Henson thanked the youngster profusely and hung up.

"Wow!" he said aloud. "Now to tackle Parker!"

Johnny was even less enthusiastic than the sports editor when the coach brought up the subject.

"Gee, coach, I'd rather not," he replied hesitantly. "I certainly was no great shakes in football here, and I'm even less of a success right now in soccer. Why not try one of the other guys? Besides, a reporter could make me sound silly. I've got problems enough without having the gang down on me as a headline hunter."

"Look, Johnny," explained Henson patiently. "This is a break for us—all of us. You're the only one on the squad who can make a real comparison between the two sports. You were a football quarterback, and now you're a goalie where you have a chance to see all the action on the field.

Besides, you're a first stringer out here, no matter what you think."

Johnny finally agreed reluctantly. "Okay, then, but what will I tell this guy?"

Mac Henson quickly sketched out some ideas. "Try to get over the idea that soccer is a game of individual skills as well as team play, too," he said. "It's teamwork that wins in both games. Too many people have the idea that it's just a sort of helter-skelter fracas with a lot of chaps scurrying about, kicking a ball wildly. And why not compare what a quarterback does with the center halfback in soccer? Tell them how a good goalie can help direct the defense. That's something for you to keep in mind, too, as you develop. And don't forget to remind them that our first game is Saturday at 3 p.m., that there is no admission charge at Watterson Field, and that the Ohio Hornets are a strong team. Tell 'em we have a better team than last year."

Still dreading the interview, Johnny said, "Please don't tell the other guys about it in advance. I don't want them riding me about it until it's over. Things are bad enough the way it is."

Johnny also was thinking of something else besides the publicity. He did not want to give Rick Weaver a chance to stir things up. If he said the wrong thing to a reporter, it could give Rick an excuse to really blast him.

"I don't know why you're so afraid of the press, Johnny," said Henson. "I know big-time college coaches can afford to be rough on reporters. Maybe they are justified now and then. I've never been in that position. But I know we need a helping hand from the student body if we're going to put our sport across. Didn't you talk to reporters when you played high school football? I understand they had some great teams where you came from."

"We did, but I had something to talk about then. I was first string quarterback on a championship team. Besides, Bloomfield wasn't a very big town. I knew the reporters personally ever since I was a kid."

"You're a first stringer now!" snapped Henson. "Don't you forget that! Unless you have confidence in yourself you may as well check out!"

"But I haven't even played in one game yet!" protested Johnny. "And here I'm supposed to be giving out interviews."

"*One* interview," said Mac Henson patiently. "And if there is any difficulty, I'll take the responsibility. All you have to do is talk!"

····· **5** ·····

Johnny Parker did not see anyone who looked like a reporter as he entered the dressing room the next day. Getting into his uniform he glanced around for Mac Henson
but the coach was not in sight. Hopefully, he thought perhaps the *Chronicle* writer had failed to show up.

After waiting restlessly for a few minutes, he went
outside to join the squad. As he glanced toward the bench
he saw Henson talking to a slender, dark-haired girl clad
in slacks and a checkered jacket. She wore heavy dark-
rimmed glasses and her hair was cut boyishly short. She
seemed to be talking earnestly to the coach, and Henson
was smiling down at her. Puzzled, Johnny stared at them
for a moment and then continued toward the far end of
the field. He had never seen a girl on the practice field
before.

Then he heard Henson's shout: "Johnny—oh, Johnny! Come over here for a moment!"

Obediently he turned back with both the coach and the girl watching him. Suddenly a chilling thought struck him. But, no, it couldn't be—not in sports.

"Miss Roberts," said Mac Henson formally, "this is Johnny Parker, the player I was telling your editor about. He's our goalie, and he's going to be a good one when he has had more experience. Johnny—Kay Roberts—she writes feature articles for the *Chronicle*. She would like to talk to you after practice if you have time."

Johnny stared at her in surprise, and then his lips tightened. A girl reporter! What was Henson trying to pull on him? It was bad enough to be interviewed by a regular sportswriter, but to answer the inane questions of a silly female, was something else. A slow burn of anger crept through him and he felt the color mount to his face.

Kay Roberts smiled and extended a slim hand. She did not seem to notice his reaction or be in the least perturbed.

"I'm glad to know you, Johnny," she said. "I hope you're not prejudiced against women reporters. I don't know much about soccer, but I'll try not to ask silly questions, and I'll do my best to learn the game."

Johnny's color deepened as he realized he had not fooled this girl. Automatically he took her hand and it felt cool and firm in his grasp. He tried to pull himself together.

"What kind of story do you want?" he asked cautiously.

Mac Henson interrupted eagerly. "Tell her about the differences you find between football and soccer. And how they are alike, too. Remember what we talked about? I'm sure you can tell her a lot of interesting things."

Standing almost behind Kay Roberts, Mac winked meaningfully. "Kay already has persuaded the *Chronicle* to let her cover Friday's game. That's a real break for us. Now let's treat her right!"

"Fine!" said Johnny, trying to keep the sarcasm from his voice. "Anything to help the press."

There was a quick glint in the girl's eyes but she said coolly, "That's the sort of thing I had in mind. Thanks, Mr. Henson."

"Just write about soccer, and don't play Johnny up too much," smiled Henson. "He's got a lot to learn."

"I'll be careful." There was an amused note in her voice as she looked at him. "Could we talk for a little while after practice, then?"

"I'll meet you here at the bench. We can sit down while we talk."

He stole a quick glance at her again as she turned to speak to Henson again. She was not beautiful but there was a wholesome quality about her, and she had poise. This was no gushing female.

Some of the other players razzed him as he took his place in front of the goal, but they also seemed impressed by the fact that their sport was getting some recognition at last.

The interview went far better than he expected. As Kay Roberts had admitted, she knew little about soccer but she was familiar with sports in general, and her questions were more intelligent than he had anticipated. Her frankness and ease of manner soon had him talking freely.

"That's about all I can think of to ask you," she said

finally. "You've been most cooperative. I hope I didn't ask too many dumb questions."

He assured her that she had not, and then he asked curiously "How come a girl knows so much about sports?"

"I have four brothers," replied Kay. "All of them played football, basketball or baseball in high school and college. When I was little they used to let me play with them sometimes. Our home could have qualified as a sports department on any newspaper."

Johnny looked at her with new respect. "If you think of anything else you wish to know, give me a call," he said.

Her eyes twinkled behind her glasses. "I'm glad you feel a little different about the interview now," she said. "I'll try to do a good job."

As she started to leave, Mac Henson strolled from the dressing room. "How goes it?" he asked.

"Fine!" they exclaimed, almost in unison.

"That well, eh?" Henson chuckled.

Johnny felt embarrassed but he saw the girl's cheeks were brighter too.

"I've got another idea, Mr. Henson. "Could I bring a photographer over tomorrow for a few pictures? Maybe I can talk the editor into a layout with the story."

"Come right ahead," said Henson heartily. "We'll be glad to cooperate with the *Chronicle*, and thanks."

The story and the photos appeared in the paper the day before the game, and Johnny was pleased at how accurately he was quoted. She had brought in the other players as well, he was relieved to see, and Henson was delighted. "That girl did a whale of a job!" he said enthusiastically. "I'm going to call her and tell her so!"

Later when he told Lockridge what the coach had

said, Vic commented, "The old boy never misses a trick, does he? Why don't you call her up, too?"

Somehow the idea pleased him, but he did not want Vic to know. "Do you think I should?" he asked doubtfully.

"From the way she looked at you," said Lockridge, "I'm sure she would be more than pleased."

"Come off it! She was just doing her job!"

"She looked like she was enjoying her work," said Lockridge with a grin.

Later when he went to the corner drugstore to call her at the *Chronicle* office, she was not there, and she did not answer at her room. He was disappointed and vaguely irritated. Women! Why the heck couldn't they stay in one place?

Johnny felt the old familiar butterflies in his stomach as he dressed for the game Saturday afternoon. This pregame feeling of weakness had plagued him throughout his high school career and he had never quite come to accept it.

This would be a new challenge in a new sport, he thought as he laced up his shoes, and he wondered if he were equal to it. He wished the nervous feeling would go away . . .

"Maybe we'll have a crowd for a change after that *Chronicle* story," said Lockridge. "That would be a switch."

If the Midwestern students had read the paper, they certainly did not respond with overwhelming enthusiasm. There were perhaps three hundred people in the weather-beaten old bleachers as the teams warmed up. Some scattered clapping and a few ironic cheers greeted them as they scattered to their positions for the kickoff.

Johnny took one quick look at the bleachers and saw Kay Roberts crouched in the front row with a pencil and notebook. A photographer with a camera dangling from a cord around his neck, left her to come down to the sideline.

The red-shirted Hornets won the toss and kicked off as the Bobcats defended the west goal. The visiting center forward tapped the ball gently to his left. Another Hornet quickly dribbled in and passed off to a fellow forward.

Suddenly Johnny saw the winger dash in to slip behind Watson as the fullback moved up to meet the Hornet attack. Then the ball came rocketing off the wingman's instep toward the goal—low and hard.

Johnny made a headlong dive and managed to cradle the ball in his arms. He rolled over and came to his feet and tossed a pass to Vic at one side of the goal. Lockridge trapped the ball with his foot, took a couple of steps forward and booted it far down the field. The Hornets dropped back to defend their own territory as Johnny heaved a relieved sigh; he had made his first save in a real game.

He saw a Hornet head the ball back, and then the center forward had it again. The red-shirted center cleverly evaded Andy Bronfeld and drove through the pack at the outer edge of the home team's penalty zone. As the ball left his foot in a low, curving arc, Johnny dropped to his knees to make the save. He flipped out to Watson, and Red booted downfield to Bob Thompson. A short pass to Weaver followed and immediately Rick and Cardenas zipped through the defense. Tony angled in swiftly to drive the ball off his left foot. The Hornet goalie could only stab at it futilely, and the Bobcats had a 1–0 lead which they kept through the first period.

Midway through the second quarter, the red-shirted Hornets broke through the Midwestern defense, but Lock-ridge managed to harass the incoming wing enough to make him kick the ball over the goal line outside of the cage.

Since the offensive team had propelled the ball across the line, the defensive team received a goal kick, and Johnny sent a long one booming almost to midfield where Bronfeld took it on his forehead and sent it lobbing toward Weaver.

But a Hornet back dodged cleverly in front of Rick to intercept the pass and the Ohio forward line came on again. A bullet smash from the center forward almost drove the breath from Johnny's lungs. He held the ball as he crashed to the turf, then flipped a roller to Watson.

Red's kick was hurried, however, and he topped the ball. A Hornet forward swooped in to trap it and lay a perfect pass in front of his right winger. The ball came in at a deceptive angle to curve into the goal at the last split-second, and the game was all tied up at 1–1.

The game seesawed through the rest of the period but there was no more scoring before the intermission. As the third quarter began the Bobcats seized the initiative but did not hold it long.

There was a spirited rally by the Ohio defense and suddenly the rugged Hornet center forward broke away up the middle, took a crossfield pass and drove in at the Bobcat goal.

Bronfeld caught up to challenge the center and the

Ohioan launched a hasty kick. Johnny crouched as the ball skidded across the grass toward him. It seemed to bound leisurely, looking big as a balloon, looking like an easy save. He took three quick strides to meet it and bent down to scoop it up. At that instant the leather took a fiendish hop over his shoulder. The triumphant shout from the Hornet bench told him what happened even before he turned around, and now the Bobcats were behind, 2–1.

Weaver raced past the goal mouth shouting, "Wake up, Parker! a ten-year-old could have stopped that one!"

Watson came over, ignoring Rick. "Don't let that upset you, chum. It took a bad hop! We'll get it back!"

Rick already was downfield lining up for the kickoff but the outburst had upset Johnny. He tried to pull himself together while a furious Bobcat drive kept the play at

the other end of the field. When Bob Thompson powered through to score, the game was all tied up at 2-all, and Johnny felt better. There was no more scoring as both defenses stiffened through the rest of the period.

The score remained tied through the forth period until there were only five minutes left. Then a Hornet back intercepted a high Bobcat pass and headed it back upfield to his own right wing. The winger dribbled along the side of the field, close to the touchline, waiting for his front-line mates to get set.

There was a quick pass to the inside left forward and a diagonal slant back to the burly center forward, and suddenly the Hornets converged on the Bobcat goal again.

In his eagerness to meet the thrust, Johnny strayed too far forward. Too late he saw the center toe a quick boot to his right forward, dash around Bronfeld, and accept the relay back from his running-mate.

Johnny tried to scramble back, expecting a shot from the right, and the center's booming shot caught him off balance. The leather shot past his waving arm to make the count 3–2 for the visitors. The jubilant Hornets danced around hugging each other as the score was posted on the scoreboard.

Although the Bobcats put on a desperate drive to tie up the match, the Hornet goalie scrambled, leaped and dove like a mad man to turn the final drive aside. The Bobcats had lost their first game. They clumped weary and discouraged into the dressing room.

"We had it and blew it," Johnny Parker exclaimed bitterly. "They shouldn't have had either of those last two goals!"

Rick Weaver did not let such an opportunity escape unnoticed. "You're so right! This is one game we should have won!"

"Listen!" snapped Lockridge. "Parker wasn't the only guy who made mistakes out there. We all did. Those were tricky shots to handle. The last one might have even slipped by Kessler!"

Johnny winced. Each of his mates, he realized, were mentally comparing him to Ernst—and the comparison found one Johnny Parker sadly lacking.

"I'll say one thing," commented Weaver. "We sure do miss that big German!"

The room grew quiet as Rick turned toward his locker, but Johnny did not reply; he knew the others all agreed.

A hand fell on his shoulder and he looked up at Mac

Henson. Here it comes, he thought, might as well get it over now.

But Henson only smiled. "Don't take it so hard, son. You played well enough except for those two shots that you might have handled if you'd had more experience. Now you've got that first one under your belt. We'll feed you a steady diet of grasscutters and bounders in practice next week."

The coach's words broke the tension. Several others spoke words of encouragement to Johnny and everyone seemed more relaxed. Suddenly he had a warm feeling for this gang; he liked them very much. They would be a good team—if he could hold up his end. Suddenly he slammed his hands together and the sound made everyone look up.

But Johnny did not speak aloud. As his jaw tightened he only told himself under his breath, "I'll make it or bust!"

Only Weaver seemed to be a sorehead. There was the Carson angle, of course, but maybe it was just that Rick was a hard loser. He tried to give the center forward the benefit of the doubt—there were worse things than hating to be a loser.

••••• 6 •••••

THE BOBCATS were scheduled to play their second game on the road, against the Castle Rock Knights, a team in an industrial city two hundred miles distant.

It was the longest and most important trip of the season since the Knights were one of the best amateur teams in their section. The Knights had generously consented to play a regulation college game with 22-minute quarters instead of two 45-minute halves, such as they were accustomed to. This test against older, more seasoned players should serve the Bobcats well for the schedule ahead, but Coach Henson still hardly expected to win. He wangled a couple of station wagons from a local automobile dealer, and the squad took off.

Castle Rock was a steel mill city and the bulk of the population was of middle European descent. The people had brought soccer with them from their native lands, and the sport flourished despite the inroads of American football and baseball.

The Knights were a brawny, formidable looking outfit in their orange shirts and black trunks. Their goalkeeper, clad in dark brown, according to the rule that a goalie's shirt must distinguish him from his mates, looked even bigger than Ernst Kessler. He was an older, partially-bald man, but he moved expertly in front of the goal.

Johnny wore a dark blue jersey in contrast to the blue and white striped shirts of the other Bobcats. He felt a brief moment of panic as he watched the Castle Rock players warm up. They seemed so confident and at ease.

The crowd was much larger than any that ever had watched the Bobcats play soccer, Lockridge commented as he glanced around at the stands.

"There must be at least five thousand people here," he said. "Imagine having a crowd like that back home!"

Henson spoke briefly before the kickoff. "Don't be overawed by these fellows," he said. "They are bigger and more experienced, but we're younger and in better condition. So let's go at top speed all the way. To them we're just a bunch of college kids—maybe we can surprise them!"

The Bobcats soon learned, however, that the Knights were too experienced and poised to be rushed off their feet. They had hard-tackling defensive backs and their center halfback covered Weaver like a blanket.

When the home team launched its own attack, the Midwestern defense had almost more than it could handle. Johnny managed to block several shots, one directly in front of the goal. Another time he leaped high to tip a ball over the crossbar, a play that brought applause from the crowd.

While the Knights put the pressure on they could not score, and the fans began to get impatient. Who did these college punks think they were? It was time to put them in their places.

The game was still scoreless with five minutes left in the first period. Then a Knight halfback stole the ball from Bronfeld and sent a quick pass to his right wing. The winger came in at top speed to fire from six yards out. Johnny tried to stretch across the goal mouth but there was too much ground to cover. The score still favored the Knights as the half ended after a scoreless second quarter.

In the third period the home team launched another attack with a series of short, accurate passes. Johnny, trying to see through the tangle of red and blue shirts before him, saw the Castle Rock center forward dribbling toward him. Anticipating a low shot, he was caught flat-footed as the ball snapped into the upper left-hand corner of the net. The Bobcats were now two goals behind.

A few minutes later, Johnny saw the ball coming at him again in a low curving arc. He deflected it back into the goal area in front of him but before he could cover the bounding ball, a Knight deftly kicked it past him and now Castle Rock led, 3–0.

Whether the home team let down because of their lead or the torrid pace, the Bobcats now began to break through the Knight's defense. Bronfeld started a drive by intercepting a long pass and volleying to Thompson. Bob fired a long cross pass to Cardenas and Tony sent the ball skipping over the goalie's shoulder to cut the lead to 3–1.

Sparked by their first goal, the Bobcats came on again. Using Cardenas as a decoy, they worked the ball to Jerry Wilson at the other wing and Jerry made it 3–2.

The Knights stormed back but Lockridge kicked the shot away to Bronfeld and Midwestern was on the prowl again. A moment later Weaver passed high to Thompson. Bob headed it past the goalie with a mighty leap and the score was tied at 3-all.

Instantly the home crowd was up imploring the Knights to come to life. But one of their halfbacks let a pass slip by him, and Cardenas was on it, tapping the ball to Weaver near the goal. Rick's path was blocked, so he sent it back to Tony, coming in on the side.

The Brazilian's speed was too great and he fired hastily. The ball struck a corner post and bounded high. The right fullback headed it far up the field. Another accurate header and the Knight center forward was inside the Bobcat defense. He shifted toward his right as Johnny leaped forward, then sent a low skipper with his left foot.

Johnny leaned forward to reach for the ball, but suddenly it bounded over his outstretched hands to give the Knights a 4–3 lead. Before the Bobcats could get rolling again, the game was over. They had lost.

Despite the defeat most of the Bobcats were not unhappy. They knew they had given the Knights a far better game than anyone anticipated. The showing gave promise of a good season despite the loss of Kessler. At least they were blessed with a strong front line, and certainly they would face few tougher clubs than Castle Rock.

Tony Cardenas, however, was inconsolable. "If I had

only taken my time on that last shot! I had the goalie beaten! If we had scored then, we might have still beaten them!"

Johnny kicked his shoes against the locker with a crash. "It wasn't your fault, Tony!" he said disgustedly. "It was mine! The ball just skipped over my hands! I still don't see how it happened—I saw it coming!"

Rick Weaver looked up from the bench where he sat taking off his shin-guards. He started to speak, then clamped his mouth shut. But Johnny got the message as their eyes met.

Back on the campus they unloaded their gear at Watterson gym and Henson said, "See you all Monday. Everyone get plenty of rest. We've got a lot of work ahead next week. My wife and I are going out of town for the weekend, so if anyone has any questions, let's have them now."

Since no one had anything to ask, the coach waved a cheery goodbye and left.

As Johnny and Vic returned to their room, the telephone began ringing. Vic answered and grinned at his roommate. "For you," he said, handing over the phone. "A nice feminine voice."

"Probably a wrong number," grunted Johnny.

"Not when she mentions you by name, buddy."

Johnny took the instrument impatiently. "Hello," he said. "Parker speaking."

"Kay Roberts, Johnny. Do you know where I can find Coach Henson? I'm supposed to do a story on the game but I haven't been able to reach him at his home or his office."

"He told us he would be out of town until Monday. Maybe he's already left."

"Oh dear! That really puts me in a bind!" She hesitated for a moment, then said, "I wonder if you could help me? Just tell me what happened over the phone?"

He glanced around at Vic Lockridge who was grinning like a Cheshire cat. "Where are you?" he asked. "I don't think I could do it from here."

"At the *Chronicle* office, but I've got to get the dope in a hurry!"

Johnny made a quick decision. "Wait there and I'll be right over. The *Chronicle* is only about five blocks from here."

"Wonderful!" cried Kay. "But please hurry!"

As he hung up he explained the situation to Lockridge.

"A new approach?" said Vic quaintly. "How do you do it, Romeo?"

"Drop dead!"

"As you will, but be sure and tell her about me."

The *Chronicle* editorial department was on the second floor of the journalism building. It was a large, untidy room with pictures, signs and huge black headlines pasted on the dingy walls. Several reporters were pecking away at typewriters, and at one end of the room a number of copyreaders were hunched over a horseshoe shaped table writing headlines. Then he saw Kay Roberts seated at a desk beneath a wall sign marked: SPORTS.

"Thanks so much for coming," she said, and motioned him to a chair beside her. "Maybe it will go faster if I just ask questions. I'll try not to keep you long."

"Oh, that's okay. I owe you that much for that fine story last week. Everybody liked it. I tried to call but you were out."

"I'm glad you liked it, and I hope the coach did, too."

"He was delighted!" replied Johnny and watched her face brighten.

She was quite attractive when she smiled.

He gave her the details of the game, and watched admiringly as she transcribed her notes into a one-page story.

"It's not very long," she apologized, "but we're crowded for space. If you can wait until I turn this in to the desk, we can have a cup of coffee in the other room if you'd like."

"Fine," he said. "I'm in no hurry now."

Over coffee Johnny told her more about the game. When he came to the goals scored against him he shook his head. "I'm afraid I'm the weak link on our club. It looks as if the other guys are going to have to score a lot of goals if we're going to win anything. The team could sure use Kessler."

Kay Roberts seemed to stiffen. "How do you expect to do anything with an attitude like that?" she asked. "You can't become a topnotch goalie all at once. Everyone has to learn."

"We've already lost two games while I'm learning. If I hadn't been such a human sieve, we'd be undefeated right now. Ernst is the big difference."

Kay's eyes flashed behind her glasses. "But Kessler isn't the goalie now—you are! It's up to you to hold up your end!"

"That's easy enough to say," replied Johnny heatedly. He was growing increasingly irritated with this girl. "I didn't become a good high school quarterback over night in high school either."

"That's a defeatist attitude," she said flatly. "You're not in high school now, and this isn't football! Why don't you snap out of it and quit feeling sorry for yourself?" Then her tone softened. "I'm sure you can handle the goalkeeper job as well as anyone if you think you can do it."

"Quit feeling sorry for myself! Who are you to talk to me like that?"

Kay flushed as she said stiffly, "I'm sorry. It really is none of my business, only I thought—" She pushed her cup aside and stood up. "Thanks, anyway for helping me. That was real sweet of you. Now if you'll excuse me, I've got more work to do."

As he left the *Chronicle* building, his anger mounted. Who did this girl think she was? Feeling sorry for himself, was he? He would show her—he would make her eat those words!

····· 7 ·····

ALL week following the Castle Rock game Johnny felt irritable and tense. In his determination to prove himself to Kay Roberts, he began to try too hard and lost his sense of timing. He missed shots that should have been routine saves.

Mac Henson studied him carefully at first and said little. Every player is entitled to an off day now and then —but by the middle of the week Johnny's sloppy play seemed to affect the whole team. The other players began to grumble and he could feel their growing hostility focus on him. Even Lockridge grew impatient.

Henson's lips tightened as Johnny let an easy shot slip through. "Come out of it, Johnny!" he called. "You should have blocked that one with your eyes shut!"

After practice, Mac called him aside. "What's bothering you, Johnny? You're getting worse instead of better.

We can't have you letting down now—not with Kent State coming here Saturday. You've got to sharpen up."

Johnny shook his head obstinately. "I'll be all right," he said. Afterward he tried to give himself a pep talk—it was time to snap out of it or call the whole thing off.

He came to the dressing room early Thursday. Maybe if he could find someone to fire some balls at him before practice he could loosen up a bit. The place was apparently deserted as he sat down quietly and began to change clothes. Then he was startled to hear voices behind the next row of lockers.

"If Parker doesn't snap out of it, we're in trouble," said Bob Thompson. "Right now it looks like the halfbacks and the fullbacks will have to carry an extra load to hold him up."

Johnny straightened up rigidly. What was this all about?

"You mean the forwards!" snapped Rick Weaver. "The only way we can win is to score more goals than he lets through! He's worse than nothing out there now!"

"Maybe we ought to talk to Lockridge, find out what his problem is," Thompson said. "It's not like him to go all to pieces this way. I've figured him as pretty solid."

"Solid!" exclaimed Weaver. "He wasn't very solid in football. According to Slade Carson he was a crybaby out there. When he saw he wasn't going to make it, he tried to twist Slade's knee and wound up with a broken collarbone instead."

"That's hard for me to believe," replied Thompson flatly. "Besides, I'm not too sold on Carson—what I've seen of him."

Before Rick could reply, Tony Cardenas said soothingly. "I don't think we should get down on Johnny. It's just a slump. But he is coming along. He will be all right. Wait and see."

"Wait!" snapped Weaver. "This guy is no better at soccer than he was at football. Now if we had Ernst—"

Andy Bronfeld spoke up. "That's hitting below the belt, Rick. After all, he's never played soccer before. We ought to try to help him—not throw rocks at him. Maybe if we all talked to him—let him know we're behind him."

"Talk to him!" sneered Weaver. "That's Henson's job! He's the coach—why doesn't he get on his tail?"

Johnny sat frozen, undecided whether to confront the others, or make enough noise so that they would realize someone else was in the room. He felt weak and nauseated at what he had heard. But he had no chance to make a decision as Mac Henson came in. The voices in the other aisle trailed away.

Henson approached him. The usual smile was missing from the coach's face. "Get out there and warm up, Parker," he said. "I'll be with you in a moment. I want to watch you work for a while. Maybe I can spot your trouble."

Johnny gladly escaped to the field. He had not meant to eavesdrop, but at least he had found out who his friends were, and what was bothering Weaver. Rick was simply Carson's stooge, and there was no truth in his accusation. He shook his head—still two strikes against him . . .

Then he upbraided himself angrily. Was he going to roll over and play dead for those two jokers? What about Cardenas, Vic, Thompson and Bronfeld? They had faith in him—he could not let them down. And what about Kay Roberts?

Mac Henson came out and sent a steady stream of kicks toward him—bounders, high shots and low ones. He was dripping with perspiration when the coach called a halt.

"That's better," said Henson. "When you relax and concentrate on what you're doing I'm sure you'll be all right. If you have some problem you want to talk over—if I can help—"

Johnny shook his head. "Thanks, Coach. I'll be all right for the game."

Saturday turned out to be a warm, sunny day, perfect for a soccer game.

The Bobcats, however, were not in a sunny mood. After they dressed they shuffled nervously as they waited for Henson to outline their strategy. As Johnny glanced around he realized the other players felt as restless and uncertain as he did himself. This was not the same team that had returned from Castle Rock, looking eagerly ahead. He glanced down at his hands and saw his knuckles white under the skin; he forced himself to relax.

"If we play the same kind of game today as we did against the Knights, we can win," said Henson. "Maybe we've just had a letdown this week. Let's forget about that now and go out and win! Kent has scored a couple of victories and they will be confident. Let's start fast and get the jump! All right—everybody out!"

As they opened the dressing room door the leading

players stared at one another. A blast of band music sounded from the field.

"Hey—what gives?" asked someone.

Henson in the rear, shouted impatiently, "Come on, shake it up! Let's go!"

They hurried down the runway to the field. A shrill burst of cheering greeted them. Four co-ed cheerleaders in uniform bounded along beside the players and motioned toward the stands. The rickety bleachers that were supposed to seat eight hundred people, were three-quarters filled.

Henson pushed through to the front of the squad. "Come on!" he shouted. "Get out there and warm up! These people came to see you play! Are you going to let them down?"

A roll of drums and the raucous blast of a trombone stirred them into action. As Johnny stood before the goal he glanced toward the stands. The band in the front row was small, but it was loud, and the musician on the bass drum seemed inspired. This was not the huge football marching band; these students were not even in uniform, but they left no doubt about it—they had come to play. Even the Kent State Mustangs looked at them curiously.

Just before the kickoff Johnny spotted Kay Roberts with the same photographer who had been with her before. They were seated at a small table behind the bench. Kay had a portable typewriter in front of her.

Henson had one last word. "I don't know who is responsible for this," he said. "But let's prove to them that we can justify this turnout."

The match started fast.

Kent won the toss and kicked off almost before

Johnny collected his wits. His eyes followed three quick passes and suddenly the Wildcat forwards were swarming in. The center forward flipped a quick pass to the left winger, and the shot came toward him waist high. He took the ball in the bread basket and wrapped his arms around it. Then Lockridge took his roll-out from one side and booted the leather down the field.

A moment later Bronfeld snared the ball away from a Mustang and dribbled down the field. A cross pass to Ron Beattie ended in an accurate header to Cardenas. Tony faked to Weaver and dribbled in. The goalie leaped out to meet him but the Bobcat forward twisted to his left and drove the ball through a corner of the goal.

The Midwestern crowd went wild at the quick goal, and the band whooped it up as the teams spread out for the next kickoff. The Bobcats led 1–0, and only four minutes of the first period were gone.

Old Watterson Field had not seen such a demonstration since the football team had moved to the stadium twenty-five years before.

The Mustangs quickly recovered their poise to put the pressure on. They attacked repeatedly, their forward line reinforced by their halfbacks. With so many players crowding the Midwestern half of the field, Johnny had to move constantly to see the ball.

Stopping that opening thrust, however, had given Johnny a mighty lift. He felt new confidence and he was sharp and quick. He hurled back two more thrusts at the goal and his long pass to Thompson opened up an opportunity for the Bobcats. But this time Cardenas' luck was bad. His shot struck the goalpost and then was deflected out of bounds off Weaver's leg.

A Mustang halfback made the two-handed throw-in, and again the speedy Kent forward line flashed in. The Bobcat defense was caught off balance by the swift-passing forwards, and before Johnny could locate the ball it zoomed toward him in a high, curving arc. He made a leaping catch and rolled to Lockridge. Vic tried to kick it out of danger, but in his eagerness the boot was too short.

The Kent left wing twisted in his tracks and sent a header rifling back past Johnny to tie the score at 1–1 as the period ended. He could only kick at the turf in disgust.

Both teams tried to put the pressure on again in the second quarter as play grew hurried and ragged. The score remained the same at the halfway mark. The home crowd did not give up at the tie score. As the team took the field to start the second half, the band and the cheerleaders helped generate a frenzy of sound.

Spurred by the ovation, the Bobcats fought furiously for the ball but the Mustangs were equally fired up. Midway through the session there was a wild mix-up, and the referee's whistle shrilled. A Kent back had stripped Weaver just inside the penalty area and Midwestern was given a direct free kick. It was a terrific break for the blue-and-white jerseyed team.

The ball was placed on the penalty mark twelve yards directly in front of the Mustang goal. All other players except Weaver, the kicker, and the opposing goalkeeper, lined up well away from the two principals. The goalie, who could not move his feet until the ball was kicked, stood tense and waiting.

Weaver sighted the shot coolly. At the moment he held an overwhelming advantage over the lone defender of the Kent nets. The Mustang netminder's eyes never left him as he advanced toward the leather.

The kick curved upward toward the right as the goalie made an acrobatic but futile leap. The ball caught in the net just beneath the crossbar and dropped to the ground and the Bobcats held a 2–1 lead.

Quickly the teams lined up for the kickoff, and immediately the Mustangs showed they were far from through. They swarmed in recklessly and there was a wild scramble in front of the home team's goal. Johnny dove instinctively toward the right, and got a hand on the ball before it spun away. As he sprawled on the turf, a cleated shoe flashed before him a dozen feet away, and he heard the ball slap into the net behind him. The score was tied 2–2. Slowly Johnny got to his feet. Pain shot through his right shoulder and he knew he must have wrenched it as he fell. Gingerly he swung his arm in a circle to test it. He moved into position still rubbing it.

"Don't worry, man!" panted Bronfeld. "We'll get it back! This is one game we're going to win!"

Weaver's slant was different. "The help we get back there!" he shouted. But he did not concentrate all of his frustration upon the goalie. He speared the ball away from a Kent wing after the kickoff. And placed it just ahead of Tony Cardenas' flying feet.

Tony shifted cleverly away from a pair of defenders who tried to force him across the touchline and out of bounds. He faked to Thompson, tapped the ball behind a defender, trapped it neatly and sent it sizzling past the stunned Kent goalkeeper.

The Bobcats were leading 3–2 as the period ended,

and although the Mustangs put on a desperate last-quarter rush, it fell short as they tired from the pace and the score remained the same at the final whistle.

When the jubilant players escaped from the crowd and headed for their quarters, someone shouted, "Hey! Where did that crowd come from? How come we rate cheerleaders and a band? What a switch!"

They were still discussing the situation excitedly as they stepped inside. Suddenly all of them stopped in amazement as they saw the tall, gray haired gentleman talking to Mac Henson in the middle of the room.

Henson turned to greet them with a smile. "Fellows, I believe all of you recognize Dr. Apperson, Midwestern's faculty representative and member of the athletic board. He wants to congratulate you on your victory."

All of them knew of Dr. Apperson, one of the great athletes of his era, a Rhodes Scholar and an Olympic hurdler who had become dean of the university's law school.

"I had no idea we had a soccer team of such caliber on our campus," Apperson said with a smile. "I often watched the game when I was a student abroad, but until today I must confess I had never seen a match in this country. But in England I learned to appreciate good play. I was curious when I saw that editorial in the *Chronicle* this morning, and I decided to see you in action. I'm glad I came."

Then the dean winked at them. "Coach Henson seems to be quite interested in varsity recognition for you men. Perhaps some have felt that he might be a bit over-enthusiastic. Speaking for myself I'm not so sure about that after what I've seen today."

Mac Henson looked puzzled. "Editorial?" he asked. "What editorial do you mean?"

"If you didn't see it," chuckled Apperson, "you had better look it up and send a note of thanks to the writer. I wonder how many others were influenced as I was, to see the game?"

When the dean had left, Henson asked, "Anybody else here see that editorial?"

Everyone had read the advance story on the sport page about the game but only Bob Thompson had read the editorial.

"It was a honey," Thompson said, "but it didn't say who wrote it."

Henson gazed thoughtfully at the player for a moment. "My guess is that the writer is a certain young lady named—" He glanced at Johnny. "What was the name of the girl who interviewed you, Parker?"

"You mean Kay Roberts, Coach?"

"Exactly! She's the one who wrote that fine feature story. Check on it for me, will you, Parker? I certainly want to thank her if she did."

Johnny felt the moisture beading on his forehead as some of the other players looked at him curiously. "Will Monday be soon enough?" he asked, trying to sound casual.

Henson chuckled. "If you are going to make a personal investigation," said Mac Henson, "I'd suggest you begin at once."

••••• 8 •••••

Back in his room Johnny reflected on the coach's words
with mixed emotions. It would be embarrassing to approach Kay Roberts after their last meeting. He still felt
ashamed of the way he had stalked out of the *Chronicle*
office but the sense of irritation also lingered. Feeling
sorry for himself, was he? Maybe the Kent game proved
otherwise. He hoped that Rick Weaver also got the message.

But as he realized what Kay had done for the soccer
club, his mood softened. The whole outfit owed her a real
debt of gratitude. Anyone who had aroused enough interest in the sport to bring Dr. Apperson to their dressing
room deserved a vote of thanks from all of them.

He glanced at his watch—might as well find out
about it now. Undoubtedly Kay would still be writing her

story at the *Chronicle*. Dialing the sport department he reached her almost immediately.

"This is Johnny Parker, Kay," he said. "I wonder if you have a few minutes to talk to me."

"Not right at the moment," she replied coolly. "I'm in the middle of a story and the deadline is coming up. What is it?"

"I'd rather talk to you personally. When can I see you?"

After a moment's hesitation she replied, "If you can make it in an hour I should be free."

"Thanks. I'll see you then."

As he put down the phone Johnny remembered that he had not read the article himself. At least he ought to know what he was talking about. He found a copy of the paper on Vic's desk and turned to the editorial page. He was surprised at the space it occupied as well as the prominent heading as he read:

ANYBODY HERE FOR SOCCER?

We wonder how many of our students realize that Midwestern has a soccer team?

Of course not many do, since it is only a club sport played by a dedicated group of young men simply for the love of the game. However, they put as much time, effort and enthusiasm into their favorite pastime as do any of the athletes in any of the so-called major sports. In fact, at most of our more prominent institutions throughout the country, soccer is a varsity sport along with football, basketball, baseball, track or swimming.

It seems to the *Chronicle* that it is time Midwestern joins the ranks of those schools that officially recognize the sport. There is an official NCAA soccer championship, and more than 500 college and university teams participate in a soccer program in addition to thousands of high schools. In some sections it ranks second only to football on an interscholastic level. Professionally soccer is being played on a coast-to-coast basis in the United States and Canada, and thousands of fans are joining the ranks of those who watch this exciting sport.

We must confess that we saw our first game only a short time ago—when the Midwestern club played the Ohio State Tech Hornets, a team that plays a regular collegiate schedule on a varsity basis. It is an exciting, fast-moving game that demands a high degree of individual skill as well as teamwork.

The rules are few and easy to learn. The field is roughly somewhat larger than a football gridiron with goals at each end. These are eight yards wide and eight feet high. There are eleven players on a side and the object of the game is to propel the ball—27 or 28 inches in circumference, weighing about one pound—across the goal line between the goal posts and under the crossbar with the feet, body or head. It cannot be thrown or carried. Only the goalkeeper may use his hands to catch or throw the ball.

Sounds simple, doesn't it? But do you know that more people in more countries of the world watch or play soccer than any other sport? Mickey Mantle would not be bugged in London for autographs, nor would the top pro-football quarterback find many receivers in Paris, Moscow or Rome. But throughout the civilized world, and some so-called uncivilized portions of it as well, the name of King Pele would be instantly recognized since the Brazilian is the greatest and highest-paid player in the world.

If you are not familiar with this fascinating sport, now is the time to find out. The Midwestern soccer club plays the Kent Mustangs, another recognized intercollegiate team on old Watterson Field this afternoon at 2 p.m. The admission is free, so why not come out and see for yourself why Midwestern should place soccer on a varsity level along with the other ten sports that represent our institution in athletic competition? You will be surprised at the action.

"Wow!" exclaimed Johnny as he finished reading the editorial. "If she wrote that Henson will recommend her for the first soccer letter ever awarded at Midwestern!"

When he arrived at the *Chronicle* office, Kay Roberts was still bent over her typewriter, frowning intently at it. She did not glance up as he came in so he leaned on the counter that separated the editorial desk from the rest of the room, and waited for her to finish.

As he watched her he shifted his elbows uneasily and wondered how to begin what he had to say. Both of them had been angry when they had last seen each other in this room. Defeatist attitude, she had said. Well, they had won the Kent game, and he knew he had played well enough. What did she have to say to that?

Then he remembered why he was there. It was really at Coach Henson's request although he had been willing, even eager, enough. Just seeing her, he thought . . .

Suddenly Kay took the sheet from her typewriter, hastily penciled a few marks on it, and looked his way. She did not smile as she lifted her hand and said, "I'll be with you as soon as I turn this in."

She returned from the copy desk a few moments later and came directly to the counter across from him. "All right," she said. "What did you wish to see me about?"

He decided to be equally blunt. "Coach Henson asked me to find out if you wrote the editorial about soccer in the *Chronicle?* He said he assumed you did."

She looked surprised as she replied, "Yes, I wrote it. Why—was there something wrong with it?"

"Wrong with it?" he exclaimed. "Mac thinks it's the greatest thing that has ever appeared in the *Chronicle!* He wanted to be sure you wrote it before he thanked you personally."

"Oh?" she said. "It's funny he didn't mention it when I talked to him after the game."

Irritated at her manner, Johnny was on the verge of telling her that he would report back to Coach Henson, and walking out. But he restrained himself and told her instead, "He didn't even know about the editorial until after the game when Dr. Apperson spoke to him about it."

Kay's eyebrows raised in surprise. "Dr. Apperson? What did he have to say?"

"He wanted to know the same thing—who wrote the editorial, and who was responsible for the band and the cheerleaders. Mac said he was sure it was you. That's why he asked me to check." Then he asked, "And you arranged for the band and cheerleaders, too?"

"I had help from the cheerleaders and also the band. Both were glad to come. I had no idea everything would turn out as it did."

"No idea!" he exclaimed. "What in the world did you expect?"

Suddenly Kay's reserve slipped away. "Johnny— when I saw that crowd, I almost flipped!"

"So did all the rest of us! You rate a gold star with Henson just for getting Dr. Apperson to the game!" He looked at her curiously. "How did you happen to get this thing about the soccer team?"

"It was really just an idea I had," said Kay. "Being in journalism and majoring in public relations, I decided to make the soccer team a project. I like sports but the only assignment I could get on the *Chronicle* was covering soccer after I wrote that feature. Some of the girls in my dorm volunteered to help, and the band director was delighted. He has just so many places in his football marching band. The soccer games will give some of his other musicians a chance to perform."

"Oh, so we're just a bunch of guinea pigs for your experiment," he said jokingly.

"It's more than that," she said seriously. "I've become quite interested in soccer. I really love to watch it, and when I went to the library to do some research I found all sorts of interesting things on the history of the game. For example, did you know that Queen Elizabeth I proclaimed that 'no football play be used or suffered within the City of London under pain of imprisonment.' What she really meant was soccer. The game was too rough and ready for the Queen's taste. It was little more than an organized gang fight."

"You ought to talk to Vic Lockridge. He's a real buff on that sort of stuff."

"The tall, good-looking fullback?" she asked innocently.

"Yeah, but forget I mentioned him, will you?"

"Nothing personal," Kay said demurely. "I was just trying to place him in my mind."

"Let's forget about him, since I'm right here. Or don't you go for short goalies?"

Kay's face tightened. "There must be thousands of short goalies in the world," she replied coldly. "If that's all you have to offer—"

For an instant Johnny sagged inwardly. He had done it again—put himself behind the eight ball with this girl he was growing to like very much. Then he straightened up suddenly. He had had enough of this humility stuff!

"I'm talking about a guy who is going to be the best goalie around—short or tall!" he snapped.

Kay smiled at him. "I read you loud and clear, man," she said. "Now how about the new goalie buying a hungry reporter a nice, thick malted?"

JOHNNY was surprised to see Ernst Kessler hobble into the dressing room on crutches before Monday's practice. While he had visited the big goalkeeper in the hospital once, time had passed so swiftly that he had not made it again.

Ernst grinned cheerfully as the squad gathered around to shake his hand.

"So you are doing well without me," he said. "That is good." He glanced down at the cast on his leg and made a face. "Six more weeks I must wear this—this thing! I'm no good for the rest of the year." He fumbled in his shirt pocket and produced a pen. "You will autograph this chunk of plaster for me, please?"

Eagerly they passed the pen around. Johnny was the last to sign the cast.

"You are now the goalkeeper," Kessler said with a smile. "How does it go?"

"I'm trying to be one," replied Johnny soberly. "I'll never be—" Suddenly he remembered his words to Kay. "I mean I hope I'll be as good as you some day." Then he added, "Next season you will be back with us."

"It is nice of you to say so," replied Ernst courteously, "but it will be a long time before I can exercise my legs, and you are gaining in experience. You have more quickness than I. It would be better if you were taller, but practice against high ones can overcome that."

Ernst manipulated his crutches toward a bench and sat down stiffly. "Me—I depend more upon height and experience, and my long arms. I have played soccer since I was eight—always a goalkeeper. I had also what you call a break. In Stuttgart we had a fine team and the greatest goalkeeper in Germany—Hans Hofner. Since he was a friend of my older brother, he sometimes came to our house. He taught me many things."

Johnny had an inspiration. "Maybe you could help me, if you are going to be out here sometimes. You could watch and tell me what I do wrong."

"Gladly, if it is all right with Coach Henson."

Mac Henson assented heartily. "By all means, Ernst. You are still a member of the team, you know, and this lad needs help."

"I will do what I can," replied Kessler simply.

During the next few days the German observed Johnny closely in practice. His criticism was kind but thorough.

"You have fine hands. You catch and throw the ball well and with accuracy. Of course, this is much different

than passing an American football—*ach*—how you people throw that slippery oval at all is beyond me!" But the objective is the same in both games—get the ball to the receiver. In soccer to his feet or head instead of his hands."

"How about low kicks?" asked Johnny. "They bother me more than high ones. The high ones I can see—it's something like pass defense in football. I'm short but I can get up in the air."

"Always advance to meet the threat when your opponent comes toward you," advised Kessler. "Try to hurry him, or force him to kick wildly. If he dribbles in or shoots from close range, then dive at the ball from five or six feet away. That's a safe distance to smother a shot. Remember, a goalie's first rule is—get the ball! One thing you must never do, except in the greatest desperation, is to try to kick the ball away. It is too easy to miss. And never dribble—pass the ball or roll it, or kick it down the field."

"How do you handle penalty shots, Ernst?"

The big German grinned as he shook his head. "More often than not—you don't. From twelve yards away no goalkeeper is faster than the ball. Besides, he must keep his feet still until the ball is kicked. One thing Hofner told me—a penalty shot kicker cannot feint. He usually aims for a spot near the goal post. Since he will not aim at you, you should stand in one corner. This will reduce the open space in front of the net and you have to move only in one direction. Of course, if you have played against the kicker before, you know whether he kicks penalty shots with his right or left foot, and whether he likes to kick high or low. As I said, no goalie can beat the ball, but he can think— and he must never give up."

The benefit of Ernst Kessler's coaching began to bring results.

Against the Westminster Deacons on the road, Johnny was robbed of a shutout by a fluky goal after the ball caromed off Watson's leg into the path of an opposing player. The Deacons were regarded as a fairly strong team and the 4–1 victory was a satisfying performance.

Only a handful of spectators were in the stands on Friday afternoon despite the Blue Jays' reputation and the Bobcat victory over Westminster.

As they came out on the field, Lockridge exclaimed, "Wow! What's happened to our crowd? There aren't a hundred people out here!"

"It just happens that the Homecoming Parade will start in half an hour," said Johnny. "Kay couldn't get any cheerleaders or bandsmen, either. Everybody's tied up. Maybe we'll get some of the alums out here when the parade is over. People are pouring into town for the big game tomorrow."

"Shows how we rate," said Vic disgustedly.

"Maybe we shouldn't cry," replied Johnny. "From what I gather, soccer games have never had even this kind of crowd before."

"I guess that's right—but now is the time we need people."

"We also need to win this game—and that's something we can do something about."

The Blue Jays were fast and tricky and they got a first period goal on Johnny to seize the lead. But the Bobcats came back to tie up the contest just before the half ended. Once more the visitors put on a burst and took a 2–1 lead in the third period. Then Tony Cardenas and Weaver swung into action. When the match was over each had two goals scored to his credit and the final count was a 4–2 victory for the Bobcats.

By the time Midwestern left the field the crowd had increased considerably in size.

"I guess they didn't completely forget us," said Lockridge. "That's something."

"You are getting the idea," said Kessler to Johnny in the dressing room. "I really have only one criticism. Do not drop to your knees in front of the ball. If you had control of your legs, they would not have scored that second goal against you. You would have been able to grab the ball before it bounced over you."

Mac Henson also was disappointed at the meager attendance. "I had an idea Dr. Apperson would bring some people to the game today, but I guess that was too much to expect with all this Homecoming business." He grinned at Johnny. "I guess it's treason to say it—but I think this school is too football-conscious."

Torrance Tech was next on the schedule and the Engineers had Mac Henson worried. "They're the best team we've faced since Castle Rock," he told the squad. "If we can get past them I'll give us a chance with Northern— and that is the one game we've got to win. That will prove without question that we're ready for the big time."

From Kay Roberts, Johnny learned that Henson also was worried on another score. Since she was regularly assigned to cover soccer for the *Chronicle*, she enjoyed the coach's confidence. Henson had not forgotten what Kay had done for his team.

"We've got to get a turn-out for this Torrance match,"

Henson told her. "We must prove that our students will support soccer. I thought we had it made when Doc Apperson showed up for the Kent game—thanks to you."

"The football team is out of town this weekend," Kay pointed out. "Maybe we can start the bandwagon rolling once more. I'm sure I can get a band and the cheerleaders. All of them had to take part in the parade last week."

"I'll try to reach Dr. Apperson on the phone," Henson said. "I'll give him my Number One sales pitch—maybe this time he can get some of the others out, too."

"What if I saw to it that a marked copy of the *Chronicle* was delivered to the offices of all board members the day before the game?" asked Kay.

"Marvelous!" cried Mac Henson. "Young lady, you're simply imspired!"

Johnny also had a problem, and it was centered around Kay Roberts. He was unable to see as much of her as he hoped to. Between studies and her daily routine at the *Chronicle*, she was a busy young woman.

Her attitude also puzzled him. Although she seemed friendly enough after their last argument, Kay never allowed their conversation to get serious. Once when he had tried to pin her down and explain his feelings she had only smiled and drawn away. "I like you, Johnny, and I value your friendship. Suppose we let things stand as they are now for a while—okay?"

Friendship! He checked the angry words that welled up inside of him. Couldn't this girl see how he felt? He forced a smile. "That's not exactly how I feel," he said, "but—okay."

"Thank you, Johnny," she said.

····· 10 ·····

WHEN the Bobcats took the field for the match with Torrance Tech, it was quickly apparent that Kay Roberts had been at work once more.

A band greeted them with a stirring fanfare. As before, what the musicians lacked in numbers they made up in volume. While the crowd did not completely fill the stands, it was noisy and enthusiastic under the prompting of the cheerleaders.

"If we don't win for this crowd," Lockridge said as they warmed up, "we deserve a swift kick—every one of us."

Johnny remained silent as the butterflies were fluttering in his stomach again. Rick Weaver's first practice shot to him whizzed by cleanly. When another caught a corner of the net above his hands, a few ironic boos came from the crowd.

"Come on, Johnny!" shouted Watson. "You're better than that!"

Gradually he settled down, but he could not shake the panicky feeling that this was not his day.

"Apperson is in the stands and there are two board members with him," said Bob Thompson as they walked over to the bench for the pre-game huddle with the coach. "That ought to give Henson a charge."

But Mac Henson was all business. "Watch for a short passing game from Torrance," he cautioned. "They like to work the ball in. They've already proved themselves defensively by holding Northern to a 2–1 score. It will take our best thus far to beat them."

The scarlet-clad Engineers were even tougher than the Bobcats expected. Their forwards were quick and fast, and ably supported by strong halfbacks who kept Cardenas, Weaver and Thompson in check.

Suddenly a lane opened in front of the Midwestern goal, and Johnny sprang out to meet the Tech center's rush. As he dove he was conscious of a scarlet flash on his left. Too late he saw the center slap the ball to the right winger. Before he could scramble back the leather was resting in the net. He caught Weaver's glare of disgust as a 1–0 lead was posted for Torrance.

Tech kept up the attack throughout the first period while Midwestern was unable to get untracked. Johnny and the two fullbacks were kept busy fending off a continuous barrage of shots. It looked as if it were only a matter of time before the Torrance team would ram home another telling stroke.

The swift pace began to tell on the Tech forwards, however, as the second period began. They were doing most of the running although the score remained unchanged at 1–0.

Then the game got rougher as the Midwestern halfbacks began to mark their opponents more aggressively, although the officials seemed to operate on a no harm, no foul rule. But when Andy Bronfeld was flattened from behind just outside the penalty zone, the referee awarded a free kick to the Bobcats.

Andy's shot penetrated the hastily formed Tech defensive wall, struck the turf in front of the goalie, and took a treacherous hop into the net to tie the score.

With less than two minutes of the half remaining, Cardenas took a cross pass from Thompson, pivoting away from a defensive back to drive the ball home again.

The Midwestern crowd went wild as the 2–1 score was marked up and they were still shouting as the period ended.

"I hope we took enough starch out of those Tech forwards to hold them the next two periods," muttered Lockridge to Johnny as they left the field. "They can really turn on the juice when they're fresh!"

Johnny nodded. "We've been mighty lucky so far. You and Watson certainly saved my neck more times than I can remember. I'm still keeping my fingers crossed this next half."

The third period proved to be even rougher than the second, and when a Tech halfback drove into Cardenas in midfield, Tony was knocked out. This time the roar of protest came from both the Bobcat players and the crowd. But a free kick taken by Thompson sailed too far to the left.

Cardenas was sent to the bench for a rest, and immediately things began to happen in the Midwestern half of the field. The Engineers mounted a determined attack and for a few minutes their front line regained its speed as it outraced the defensive halfbacks again to let Johnny, Lockridge and Watson bear the brunt of the assault.

Vic kicked one shot aside and Watson broke up a cross pass. But before he could boot the ball out of danger, the left winger stole the leather and sent a backward pass to his center who was coming in at full speed. Johnny was caught off balance by the clever maneuver as the center scored from half a dozen yards out to tie the score at 2–2.

Weaver came raging back. "Get with it, Parker! This is no place to take a nap!"

Johnny was angry and frustrated enough by his mistake—if it had been one. He felt he had taken the only chance open to him but he had not reacted quickly enough.

"How about getting some goals yourself?" he yelled back at Rick. "You guys are letting them take the play away from you!"

Lockridge came over beside him. "Easy, Johnny," he panted. "We can't get anywhere jawing at each other!"

Still smoldering inside, Johnny bent over. "Weaver and his big mouth," he said.

Both sides started quick rallies as the final period began, but they soon subsided. The grinding pace was telling on the players.

Then as the fleeting moments of the game were ticking off, the Bobcat forward line closed in on the Tech goal once more. But a defensive half intercepted a pass to Cardenas, who had returned to the game, and promptly kicked it to midfield. A Torrance forward beat Bronfeld to the ball and came dribbling into the Bobcat penalty zone.

Andy forced him to shoot hurriedly from far out, however, and Johnny easily caught the ball. He rolled it off to Watson, but Red took his eyes off the leather and his kick was a weak roller that a scarlet-jerseyed forward quickly gobbled up.

The Bobcat defense scrambled wildly to protect their goal. Johnny danced back and forth as the ball was screened from him by the milling throng. But he saw the leather in time to take it on the chest and cradle it.

As he turned to flip the ball safely to Vic Lockridge, his eye caught Rick Weaver down the field, waving his arms and shouting. He glanced once more at Lockridge, hesitated, and turned to hurl the ball toward the Bobcat center forward.

But as he shifted the leather in his sweaty hands, he juggled it for a moment and then threw it wildly. Instantly he knew the throw was short and late; Rick already was crossing the midfield stripe.

A Tech player leaped high to head the ball back to a mate deep in the Midwestern penalty zone. The Torrance forward saw Johnny moving toward him, and jumped up to meet the ball with another header that shot downward into the unprotected Midwestern goal.

As the jubilant Tech players shouted and pounded each other, Johnny stood staring blankly at the ball resting quietly in the net.

Lockridge seized him by the arm. "What in the world were you thinking about? Why didn't you give it to me?"

"I—I thought Weaver called for it! He was open!"

Vic stared. "For the love of Pete, Johnny! This was no time to take a chance like that!"

The Bobcat fans sat stunned as they watched a joyful Tech player seize the ball a minute later and race off the field. The match was over and Midwestern had lost 3–2. The game had been decided upon one stunning misplay. Even students who did not understand soccer knew that the Bobcat goalkeeper had goofed.

Johnny looked up as Rick Weaver ran toward him. Rick's face was hot and angry. "Were you out of your mind, or something?" he demanded. "Throwing the ball away like that!"

"I thought you were signaling me to pass to you," replied Johnny. "You waved your arms and shouted something about being wide open! What about that?"

"I signaled you! Are you kidding? I was hollering for the rest of our line to get into position. Everybody was back on defense—trying to protect you!"

"But I thought—"

Weaver's eyes were hard with suspicion. "Don't use me for your alibi! Don't try to pin the blame on me!"

Rattled and fatigued, Johnny tried to think of something to justify his action but neither thoughts nor words would come.

Rick started on, then turned suddenly. "And you were the guy who thought he was a quarterback! Man—oh— man!"

Lockridge fell in beside Johnny as they walked to the gym door. "I didn't mean to be so hard on you," he said. "Everybody makes mistakes. This isn't the end of the world, you know."

Johnny stared at him bleakly without replying. What was the use? The answer was obvious; he was a born blunderer, and had been all the way.

Inside, the players were glowering and silent. It had been a tough one to lose. Johnny went to his locker, head down, hoping nobody else would speak to him. He had had enough.

Then he was conscious of Mac Henson, standing beside him, the tiredness and the tension still on his face. There was bitterness in his eyes but his voice was quiet and controlled.

"How do you explain what happened out there?" he asked. "I'm afraid I don't understand."

Johnny told him, not really caring if he sounded convincing or not. When he finished there was an uncomfortable silence.

Then Henson said, "I see. The long football forward pass, eh? Well, as we all saw—it did not work. Hereafter, let's stick to soccer, since that's what we are supposed to be doing." As an afterthought, the coach went on, "Aside from that one bonehead play, you did well. You deserve that much credit, at least."

Tony Cardenas was the only one who did not act as if he was attending a funeral. The little Brazilian flashed his quick, bright smile.

"Tough, Johnny—very tough! The bad break today— the good one tomorrow. You remember that!"

"Oh, sure, Tony," replied Johnny as he picked up his towel and headed for the shower.

····· **11** ·····

WHEN Johnny returned to his room he found Vic Lockridge dressing hurriedly for a date.

"Too bad you can't come along," Vic said, "but it's too late now. Do you good to get out and forget the game. Don't let it get you down."

"Don't worry," replied Johnny shortly. "It won't."

Lockridge left a few minutes later with a cheery goodbye, and for a while Johnny felt relieved. But as he stared through the window at the gray twilight, the quiet room seemed to become lonely and cheerless. Gathering his books together, he slammed the door behind him. Anything was better than to sit there brooding.

Although he was not particularly hungry, he grabbed a snack in the dormitory cafeteria and luckily ran into no one who had seen the match. He felt much better as he headed toward the library.

The huge reading room was almost deserted at this hour. Resolutely he laid out his books on a table, and told himself this was a great time to get some work done. But soon the brooding stillness got on his nerves, and he stood up and walked to the water fountain in the hall. When he returned it was just as hard to concentrate as it had been before.

His watch told him it was seven-thirty and he wondered if Kay Roberts was at the *Chronicle*, writing her story of the game. Usually she ate dinner first, since the paper's deadline was eleven o'clock.

Johnny closed his books for the second time that evening. Then he headed for the newspaper office. He wondered what Kay's reaction would be to the boner that had lost the game, but at least he could talk to her; besides he was curious about what she was going to write.

Kay greeted him with a smile. "And how does the martyred hero feel?" she asked.

"Ouch!" he said, forcing a grin. "I guess I shouldn't expect tea and sympathy tonight."

"Only black coffee," she said briskly, "and it will have to be quick. I'm due at the hospital at eight."

"At the hospital! What in the world for?"

"I've taken a job as night receptionist for the next two weekends to fill in for the regular girl who is on vacation. The money I can use."

"You mean you're leaving the *Chronicle*?" he asked in quick dismay. "You won't be writing about us any more?"

"Oh no," she replied. "I'll cover soccer. But now I'll have to do my story and run. Come on, we'll raid the coffee urn before I leave."

"Well, what did you think?" he challenged as they drew their coffee. "Am I a rockhead, or not?"

"Only in your own mind as far as I'm concerned," Kay replied. "You might have been like the football quarterback who hurls the last minute pass for a touchdown—if what I think you had in mind had succeeded."

He stared at her for a moment in silence. What she had said provided him with a perfect out, and it would look good in print. "Did you write it that way?" he asked.

"Not exactly, but I mentioned the possibility."

"Maybe you had better change your story. It didn't happen that way at all. I goofed. I should have passed off to Lockridge. I thought that Weaver was calling for the ball, but he said he was trying to get the forwards down the field. Everybody was back on defense."

Kay frowned at him. "Are you sure? I was certain I heard him call for the ball. Of course, there was so much noise, I could be wrong."

"That's not what he told me."

"Maybe I had better change that paragraph. It would just mean cutting out a line."

"I think you had better. Besides, I don't want to make it look like an alibi."

She excused herself and hurried back to the editorial room. In a moment she returned. "Thanks for telling me."

Johnny walked with her to the hospital entrance, and all the way she remained preoccupied and silent.

"A penny for your thoughts," he said as they arrived at the door.

"It worries me," she said. "I thought I distinctly heard Rick shout, "This way, Parker! Pass it to me!'"

"I guess it doesn't make any difference now. I should

have been smart enough to pass to Lockridge, anyway. That was the conservative thing to do."

"Probably—only—" Kay placed a hand on his arm. "Anyway, thanks for correcting my story."

There were only two games remaining on the Midwestern schedule now. The first was a Friday contest against the Tareyton Indians, and the next week would be the big one—the final match of the season—against the Northern State Falcons.

Although the Indians had been a disappointment to their followers by losing five straight, they had won their last two starts against good opposition. Mac Henson warned his team not to expect an easy match.

"We must guard against the danger of looking too far ahead," he cautioned. "I know you want to beat the Falcons more than anybody else. Not that you should be overconfident against the Indians, after last week's match."

He glanced around the dressing room and Johnny winced.

"But we must remember that our sport is like any other," he continued. "We play only one opponent at a time, and anything can happen. It's the game just ahead that's the big one, no matter who it is. Don't ever forget that. All things being equal, it's usually the team that is better prepared mentally that wins."

The Bobcats went through their practice paces at a surprising clip all week. Johnny was both pleased and relieved that none of the other players, particularly Weaver, had brought up his unfortunate performance against Torrance Tech again.

He wondered about Rick after what Kay had said, but as she admitted, she could have been wrong during all the noise and excitement. Her story had not been generous but it had been fair, and nobody could accuse her of alibiing for the goalkeeper or the team.

Whether Henson's warning had its effect, or whether the Bobcats were especially sharp, they passed and shot their way to an easy 5–1 victory over the Indians. Weaver and Cardenas scored in the first period and Thompson added another in the second, to give the home team a 3–0 lead at the half.

The visitors' center forward broke through in the third period to score his team's lone goal on a low shot past Johnny. But the Bobcats scored twice in the final quarter to produce a satisfying 5–1 victory.

"That was more like it," said Lockridge afterward. "If we can be as sharp as that next Saturday, we'll give those Falcons all they can handle."

As they ate their dinner at a campus restaurant, they watched a TV news program. When it ended the news shifted to a sports show and suddenly the Midwestern football coach, Mike Armstrong, appeared beside the sportcaster to talk about tomorrow's game against Wisconsin.

"That reminds me I haven't seen a football game this year," said Lockridge. "This looks like a good one. Why don't we go together?"

Johnny sat uncertainly for a moment. Then he said, "I haven't seen one either and I don't know as I care to start now. Besides, I didn't buy a student ticket."

"Oh, come off it!" urged Vic good-naturedly. "So you didn't make the team and you're playing soccer. That isn't the worst thing that could happen to you. If it's a ticket you're worried about, I've got a pair. The date I had struck out on me."

"I could use the time studying," objected Johnny half-heartedly.

"You can always use the time studying—even when you're asleep. Come on—I'm offering you a free ticket. Don't be a jerk!"

"All right. If that's the way you feel. Thanks."

..... **12** .....

SATURDAY dawned bright and sunny, a perfect day for a football game. A cool northwest breeze stirred the pennants around the upper rim of the Midwestern stadium as the morning sun warmed the red brick walls.

This much Johnny Parker saw as he hurried to his first hour class. Not enough wind to affect the kicking or the passing, but brisk enough to keep the air stirring down on the gridiron. It could get hot down there on a sunshiny afternoon.

Despite his earlier vow to forget about football, he felt a little thrill of anticipation run through him as he thought about the game.

This inner excitement grew after lunch as he and Vic joined the slowly moving stream of fans heading toward the stadium gates. The seats were excellent, high and almost on the forty-five yard line.

It had been a long time since he had watched a game from the stands. He had always played in high school, and last year the freshmen squad sat on a bench behind the varsity.

It was strange that he felt no qualms as the teams warmed up. What seemed stranger, however, was to see the figures down on the field throw passes, catch thrown passes and run with the ball in the close-knit offensive formations—so unlike soccer. He was amazed that in so short a time the game he had always known had come to seem so different.

Then his eyes focused on Number 26—Slade Carson. There was no mistaking that big, fast and graceful figure with the buggy-whip arm. The close-fitting blue jersey and the tight yellow pants made him look trim and lean.

As the game began he was surprised to realize how slow it seemed to him. The huge lines charged and tussled, and there was more delay between plays than he remembered. The huddle, the shift, the quarterback's count— had it always been this slow?

"That's funny," he said aloud.

"Yeah?" Lockridge eyed him quizzically. "What's funny?"

"It seems so slow."

Vic grinned. "I've been thinking the same thing. Soccer seems a lot faster."

"It sure does!" Johnny replied, wonder in his voice.

Gradually, however, as he became absorbed in the action he lost this sense of slowness. Despite his feeling against Carson, he had to admit the big quarterback was doing a superb job.

As the game seesawed back and forth during the first

half, Carson's slashing runs and accurate passes alone kept the Bobcats in the contest as Wisconsin drove to a 16–14 lead at half time.

"You may not like Carson personally," said Vic as they watched the Midwestern band march out on the field, "but to my way of thinking, he is an All-American if there ever was one. I don't know too much about football, but I think he's great!"

"I hate to admit it, but you're right," replied Johnny. "When I see the way he's playing now, maybe I shouldn't feel so bad. If only he wasn't such a heel."

"You're learning," grinned Lockridge. "You stick to soccer and you'll be better off."

Early in the third period Slade threw a 40-yard surprise pass that the Bobcat left end hauled to the seven-yard stripe. On the next play Carson faked a dive into the line and cut back off tackle to score. He was hit at the two-yard stripe by two massive linebackers but this momentum carried him into the end zone.

Then Johnny and Vic joined the Bobcat fans as they leaped to their feet. Slade Carson lay writhing on the ground as the officials untangled the pile-up. The trainer ran out, then the coach. The quarterback was carried off the field on a stretcher.

As the play was resumed, there was only a token cheer for the touchdown and the extra point. Everyone in the stadium was watching the stretcher disappear into the tunnel that led to the dressing room.

Without Slade Carson directing things for the home team, the Badgers soon regained the lead. The final score was 23–21, with Wisconsin threatening to score again.

"What a way for the game to end!" exclaimed Vic in

disgust. "And what a tough break for Carson! I hope it's not too serious."

Before Johnny could reply, some spectator further down toward the playing field shouted, "They say they've taken Carson to the hospital! He might have to have an operation!"

Johnny found himself feeling sorry for Slade Carson —a thing he never would have believed could happen. Even though he recalled vividly the jeering remarks and the riding he had taken from the cocky athlete, he felt pity for him now. Slade had played a fine game and he had had a great season. In retrospect he saw that he had been foolish ever to have believed he could displace Carson at the signal-calling post.

As the two boys returned to the dormitory they heard more details on the injury over the radio. The Midwestern team physician was quoted as saying that it looked like a torn cartilage in the right knee, but until the X-rays had been studied, no official statement would be forthcoming.

Later when Johnny tried to reach Kay at the *Chronicle*, the reporter on the sports desk was impatient with him.

"Look, buddy, we're swamped with calls on this thing," he said. "All we know is that X-rays will be taken. Be a nice guy and hang up so we can get our work done."

When he also failed to reach her at the hospital, he gave up in disgust.

The story on Slade Carson was in the papers and on all the newscasts Monday morning. The Midwestern quarterback would undergo knee surgery before the day was over. This meant he definitely was through for the season.

Strange how things worked out, Johnny mused as he

heard the sportscast. Only a few months ago he was fighting desperately for a chance to play quarterback for the Bobcats himself. He had not only been beaten out, but humbled and sneered at by Carson, a player who had too much ability to stoop to such petty things.

Now it was Carson who had been knocked off his glory perch by a single bad break, while he, Johnny Parker, faced a crisis in a different sport.

Although no title aspirations depended upon his performance, he knew that the hopes of Mac Henson and the entire soccer squad might hinge upon his showing against the Northern State Falcons on Saturday afternoon. How well he met the challenge could mean varsity letters for all of them next year.

His brow creased in a frown as he stared down at his hands. There also was the matter of his self-respect, and the respect of his fellows, not to mentioned that of a girl named Kay Roberts.

Johnny did not see Kay again until he accompanied her from the *Chronicle* to the hospital two nights before the game.

"We never get a chance to talk any more since you took this job," he complained as they arrived in the lobby. "It used to be more fun when you just worked for the *Chronicle*."

Kay glanced around the room. "Looks as if it's going to be a quiet night," she said. "Why don't you bring up a chair and sit by my desk? That way it will look as if I'm receiving an incoming patient. If I really get busy you can just get up and leave."

"Great!" cried Johnny. "I'll give you more symptoms than a whole ward full of patients!"

She looked at him in alarm. "Keep your voice down! Here comes someone now."

Johnny stood up hurriedly and turned around to face Mike Armstrong, the Midwestern football coach. He hoped that Armstrong would not recognize him but the coach's face broke into a broad smile.

"Well, if it isn't little Johnny Parker!" he boomed. "Where have you been keeping yourself, son? Just because you joined this soccer club is no reason why you can't pay us a visit now and then. I suppose you're up here to see Slade—the poor guy! I just came from there. I'm sure they'll let you in."

Johnny's mouth dropped open. Either the coach had a short memory or there were some things he never knew. Imagine he, Johnny Parker, coming up to the hospital to see Carson!

The coach's smile, however, was so genuine and friendly, that Johnny felt embarrassed.

"Yeah," he said rather vaguely. "I'll try to do that." He saw the quick gleam of amusement in Kay's eyes. Why didn't Armstrong say goodbye and get on his way?

"Be seeing you, son." The big man waved a hand. "Carson will be glad to see you. Try to cheer him up. The poor kid is really down." He smiled at Kay. "So long, Miss."

As Armstrong breezed out through the front door, Johnny glared after him, then turned to Kay who was trying to suppress her laughter.

"He's certainly a friendly man," she said.

"And a forgetful one," replied Johnny. Then he sighed. "But I guess he can't be expected to remember every little squabble among his players."

"Little squabble!" Kay's eyes shone mischievously. "When you first told me about it I thought it was one of the major incidents in your life!"

Johnny shifted uncomfortably. "Funny, how it doesn't really rate so big now," he said. "Getting practically kicked off the football squad seemed like a major tragedy at the time. And Slade Carson didn't make it any easier. I don't think I owe him very much."

Kay looked thoughtful and then she said, "Why not go up and see him? It wouldn't hurt to stick your head in and say hello."

"He'd probably make some smart remark and think I was crazy."

"Could be," Kay said slowly. "Could be that it would show him you're a bigger man than he is, too. Have you thought of that?"

Johnny considered her words for a moment. "You really think so?"

"He might really appreciate it. If he doesn't—so what? He would only prove that he's the kind of a heel you think he is."

"I'll do it," Johnny said abruptly. "I'll be right back."

Kay looked up the room number for him and Johnny took the elevator to the fifth floor. He started down the long hall looking for 525B.

Suddenly he stopped in his tracks. Coming out of a room two doors down was Rick Weaver. Rick's eyes widened and he, too, hesitated.

"Hi," he said.

Johnny recovered first. "That's Carson's room you just came from?" he asked.

"Yeah," he said, "but—"

"Thanks."

The surprised look did not fade from Weaver's face as he hurried toward the elevator bay.

Cautiously, Johnny looked into the room. Slade Carson was propped up in bed, his heavily bandaged knee propped up before him. His astonishment was even greater than Rick's when he saw his visitor.

"Hello, Slade," said Johnny. "How's it going? Sorry to see it happen."

An ugly light appeared in Carson's eyes as he stared at his visitor. "What brings you here?"

"Nothing in particular." Johnny tried to sound casual. "I was up this way and I thought I'd wish you luck. I saw what happened at the game."

Slowly the suspicion faded from Slade's face. A dull red color crept into his cheeks. "Well—uh—thanks, Parker." He laughed uncertainly. "I hardly expected to see you."

Suddenly he grimaced as he shifted in bed. "Ouch! That blamed knee is acting up again."

Before Johnny could reply, a nurse came briskly into the room. "Visiting hours are over for you, young man," she said to Carson with a smile. "Time to take your temperature, and see that you get a good night's rest."

"So long then," said Johnny. "I hope everything turns out okay."

"Thanks for coming," mumbled Slade around the thermometer. "Nice of you."

As Johnny went down the hall his step was quicker, and he was surprised at how good he felt.

When he reached Kay's desk again, she got the message with one glance at his face and smiled. "Well, it wasn't too difficult, was it?" she asked.

He told her what had happened, including his meeting with Rick Weaver. "I'm glad I went up there now," he said. "Thanks for suggesting it."

"I'm glad you did, too, Johnny," Kay said. "It's time all three of you grew up."

····· **13** ·····

Mac Henson was already in the dressing room when the Bobcats arrived for Friday's final workout. His face was solemn and intent as he paced restlessly in front of the lockers. He did not speak until everyone was in uniform.

"We've come a long way since our first game," he began quietly, "and now it's almost zero hour—time to see if our dream will come true. You fellows have done a terrific job, and I hope that by this time next season you will have earned your varsity letters—those of you who will be back. But for those of you who are seniors you have the satisfaction of knowing that you have helped make the athletic board sit up and take notice."

He paused for a moment, and then continued. "Dr. Apperson told me last night that he is all for us. He's bringing enough members to the game tomorrow to swing the vote in our favor, if they like what they see.

"There is one other thing I would like to bring up. Our good friend from the *Chronicle* called to say that we'll have a bigger band tomorrow than ever before, and we'll have the same cheerleaders to help. And about that girl, Kay Roberts, I think we should do something special for her. How many of you would like to chip in with me and buy her a present—maybe a ring or a bracelet—something to show our appreciation. All in favor say aye."

There was a unanimous murmur of assent, and the coach said, "Fine. Johnny, you and Vic collect the money and pick out the present."

Lockridge spoke up quickly. "I'll be glad to help collect, but I'm lousy at picking out presents for women. How about Johnny taking care of that department? After all, he should know better than any of us what she might like."

A quick chorus of laughter greeted Vic's suggestion as Johnny glowered at him.

"Okay, you're appointed official buyer, Parker," said Henson. "We'll present it to her at a party I'm giving for the squad next week." Then the coach became serious once more.

"We all know what we're up against tomorrow," he continued. "We haven't trimmed Northern since they went to the final round in the NCAA championships three years ago. Let's prove that we're ready for the big time by giving them a beating. Nobody can deny us if we can do that! What do you say, gang?"

The answering shout made the lockers rattle in the shabby old dressing room.

They went out to the field and warmed up briefly, then Henson sent them in. "Keep off your feet as much as possible tonight and get a good night's sleep. Everybody back here by one o'clock tomorrow."

As they trotted up the runway, Johnny felt a tap on his shoulder. Rick Weaver said, "I'd like to speak to you for a minute, Johnny—alone."

Johnny hesitated for an instant before he replied, "Okay," and stepped to one side. "What's on your mind?"

Weaver seemed embarrassed. "Look, Johnny," he said. "I don't know how to say what I mean, and maybe it isn't even any of my business—but that was a pretty decent thing you did last night. I guess I had some wrong ideas about you, and I'm sorry. I talked to Slade before I came to practice, and he admitted he was prejudiced, just like he is with anybody who might give him competition. But you really surprised him and made him feel ashamed. He's cocky and hard-headed but he's got some good points, too. Anyway, he asked me to wish you luck tomorrow."

"He said that?" asked Johnny gruffly. He did not want Rick to see how he felt. Then he put out his hand. "All right, Weaver, and thanks to both of you."

Rick did not accept the hand immediately. "There's one thing more," he said slowly. "About that Torrance game—I really did holler at you. Then when things went sour, I let you take the blame. I've felt like a heel ever since it happened but I didn't have the guts to tell you. I'll go to Henson if you want me to."

Johnny's face froze, and he started to turn away. But he turned around again. "I'm glad you told me," he said slowly. "It's bothered me a lot but I'm glad you told me. Forget about Henson."

Then he added with a slow grin. "It still would have been a good idea if it worked."

Rick seized his hand, and they went inside together. Johnny felt even better than he had the night before. He was really one of the gang now—the whole gang.

····· **14** ·····

Tʜᴇ Northern State Falcons left no illusions about their prowess from the opening moments of the Midwestern game.

Immediately after the kickoff they powered their way deep into Bobcat territory, and Buff Dixon, their star center forward, launched a terrific kick from eight yards out that Johnny Parker could only slap at as it whizzed past. The ball dented the net so deeply that it stuck there until the referee jerked it loose.

Johnny bent over, hands on knees, blinking dazedly as the official trotted back to midfield to place the ball for the next kickoff. Within two minutes the green-jerseyed horde was swarming the Midwestern penalty zone again, scattering the halfbacks like chaff before the wind.

The Bobcat bleachers, so tightly packed that the

crowd overflowed along both touchlines, shrieked wildly at the team to get going. Suddenly the ball shot out of a revolving mass of players toward the goal. This time Johnny managed to get in front of it to hug it tightly until he could push it to Vic Lockridge. Vic sent a low, hard kick out to midfield.

Within seconds the nightmare began once more. Johnny covered one attempt with a long dive, blocked another and sent a long throw to Bronfeld. Andy's cross pass was intercepted by a Falcon who headed it to Dixon. The Northern center sent a short kick to his left half.

In his eagerness Johnny came out too far, and again a Falcon goal was chalked up to make the score 2–0 against Midwestern with the game barely five minutes old.

"Come on, you halfbacks!" shouted Lockridge. "Let's be alive up there! Get that ball!"

Gradually the defense braced to slow down the Northern attack. But Dixon seemed to be everywhere both on offense and defense. Midway in the period a team-mate slapped the ball in front of the green-shirted center forward and he came in swiftly from the left as Johnny prayed that one of the backs would mark him.

But the Falcon feinted Watson out of position and dribbled around him. Johnny could only move out to meet the challenge. Even as he dove, Dixon pivoted smoothly and shot the ball past the Bobcat goalie once more. Johnny felt weak and sick as he got to his feet. This was no soccer game; this was a slaughter! Now the period was little more than half over and the Falcons had a three-goal lead.

Then the Bobcats began to fight back. After the kick-off Weaver made a brilliant tackle on Dixon and sent the ball to Tony Cardenas. Tony skillfully pushed it back to Ron Beattie, and the Englishman relayed a quick pass to Weaver.

Rick's shot struck a goal post and bounded back high in the air. Bob Thompson leaped and headed it into the net just beneath the crossbar. For the first time the Midwestern stands had a chance to roar their acclaim.

Three times in quick succession the front line moved in with short passes. Twice the Falcon goalie blocked and cleared successfully. The third attempt struck a post again and the brawny Northern right fullback sent a tremendous boot that rolled into the Bobcat half of the field. The score remained at 3–1 as the first period ended.

Lockridge and Weaver ran around trying to rally the team during the brief intermission and Johnny began an encouraging chatter from in front of the goal.

"Stick with it, gang!" urged Vic. "We'll catch up with 'em!"

"Let's keep our passes short," said Weaver. "We've got to keep the ball away from them. Don't try any long ones unless you're sure your man is clear!"

Halfway through the second period the Bobcats got a penalty shot when a Falcon forward charged into Johnny, knocking him back into the net.

Weaver took the shot and booted it perfectly, a rising drive that completely fooled the Falcon goalkeeper. The Midwestern stands came up with a long shout as the 3–2 score was posted.

The goal against them seemed to spark a comeback for Northern State. They put on a tremendous rush, and suddenly the ball slipped from under Johnny as he tried to dive on it. The Falcons had regained part of their advantage, and the score was still 4–2 as the half-time mark was reached.

Mac Henson's face was white and strained but his voice remained calm. "Whatever you do, don't give up!" he urged. "You survived that opening blitz, and you're still in the game. Watch out for a quick starting rush—they'll figure a quick goal now will put the match on ice. Let's cross 'em up and get one ourselves! That will chase 'em back on defense and give us a chance to run. Bronfeld, I want you to mark that Dixon fellow so tightly that you'll leave a brand on him! Stop him and you can win!"

Both sides tried the quick goal strategy that Henson had mentioned as the third quarter opened, but neither was successful. The Falcons seemed willing to conserve their strength and protect that 4–2 lead.

"Their right halfback is either tired or he's loafing," Cardenas muttered to Weaver. "Next time you get the ball, give it to me. I can get around him. If I can't get inside I'll pass back to you in the middle."

When Weaver got the ball he dribbled forward, evaded a Falcon with a quick shift while watching Cardenas from the corner of his eye. As Tony broke into a serving dash, Rick laid the ball in front of him. The Brazilian half pint was moving at top speed as he angled it on the goal.

Weaver tore down the middle area shouting, "Over here, Tony! Give it to me!"

The Falcon goalie heard the shout and took his eyes off of Cardenas for an instant. Tony's shot came in low and hard in that split-second. The ball nestled into a corner of the net and the score was 4–3, as the Bobcats gathered around Tony, shouting wildly.

A change was quickly made in the Northern State strategy. The defensive backs no longer crowded up to support their forwards so closely. A sub was sent in for the erring halfback who had let Cardenas get away.

Tony proved the perfect decoy now. He baffled the new player with his tricky feints and dashes while Weaver, Beattie and Thompson worked the ball through the Northern penalty zone. Nothing came of the thrust, however, as Bob's shot sailed wide of the mark. The Falcon goalkeeper sent the goal kick from the right side of the penalty zone with a boot that even drew applause from the Bobcat followers.

Another Falcon managed to reach the ball before Midwestern could head it away. He flicked a quick pass to one side and the smooth-working Northern line took over with a rush.

A wave of green-clad attackers bore down on Johnny but he managed to stave off two drives and clear the ball each time to his fullbacks.

When the Falcon line surged in a third time, he sent a lobbing kick over the rushing players. He noticed that the halfbacks were crowding up again as the ball bounded and rolled deep into the opposing penalty zone before a fullback rushed out to boot it out of danger.

The play set Johnny thinking. What if Weaver or Cardenas had reached the ball first? Or if he had passed directly to Rick, running ahead of the pack? It would be something like that unlucky play against Torrance, but what if they set it up deliberately? But Henson would crown him if he took a chance like that again.

He had no further time to think about it as the Falcons closed in again. Suddenly he dove, came up with the

ball and flipped it to Watson. Red relayed it to Bronfeld, who sent it down to Jerry Wilson. Wilson's shot was deflected by the goalie to a Falcon fullback. But the Northern player fumbled it and it rolled back across the goal line to give the Bobcats a corner kick.

Weaver sent the kick across the goal mouth about ten yards out but the Falcons were bunched tightly in front of the net and Thompson headed it back toward midfield. The Northern players moved out to follow the play and there was a scramble before Thompson sent a cross kick toward Cardenas who went flying in. Tony trapped it, took two strides and drove the ball off his left instep for the tying score. The period ended a moment later with the match standing at 4–4.

As the teams changed ends of the field for the last quarter, Johnny called Rick and Cardenas to him. "I've got an idea," he said. "Maybe we can set up something for these guys."

Both forwards listened intently as he outlined his scheme. "Something like the Torrance game," he said. "Only this time Weaver takes the pass if the defense pulls up toward midfield like they have been doing. If you cross to Tony as he comes down from the left, Rick, that goalie is going to be in deep trouble with no help back there."

"But so would we, Johnny!" protested Cardenas. "I could be offside unless there are two defensive players between me and the goal line."

"Not if you take the pass with two players between you and the goal line—you can shoot from any place you want to. Just be sure you take the ball from Rick while two Falcons are down there—the goalie and any other player would be enough."

"That's right," said Weaver quickly. "I'll start dribbling in from one side and as the defense catches up I'll
pass back to you diagonally. There won't be any question
about it—and you go in at full speed."

"Let's go then!" cried Tony excitedly. "What do we
wait for?"

"Easy," cautioned Johnny. "I've got to get the ball first
and you've got to know when I'll pass it."

"We'll be watching you," Weaver said. "I'll go down
on the right the first time they get in for a shot. When you
throw, you yell at the top of your voice. Then I'll turn on
the steam. Tony—you know what to do?"

"*Si—yes!* I know!"

It was time to resume play. The Falcons immediately
put on the pressure. Twice Johnny took the brunt of their
drives as the Bobcat halfbacks failed to mark Dixon
tightly enough. For a moment he had a dispairing thought;
it would be only a matter of time before Northern scored
again if he did not get more help.

The ball came smashing in a third time. Lockridge
kicked it aside and Bronfeld managed to send it back almost to midfield with a quick boot. But a Falcon leaped in
front of Thompson to kick the ball away and in a moment the penalty area was flooded with green shirts again.

Johnny's eyes were on Buff Dixon, the center forward,
as the whole Falcon team seemed to be rushing at him. He
saw Dixon take a pass from the left, and suddenly the ball
was coming in like a bullet. At the last split second he left
his feet in a long dive and crashed to the turf, clutching
the leather tightly. He rolled over and came to his feet,
glancing instinctively toward Lockridge.

It was then he saw that the Falcons were still

bunched in front of the goal. He caught a glimpse of Weaver running in the clear, one hand raised. He took three quick steps and hurled the ball down the field as he yelled, "Now!"

The leather sphere struck the ground ahead of Weaver and bounded once before Rick trapped it and dribbled forward a few strides. As his marking back caught up with him, he shot a diagonal cross back to Cardenas who was running easily on the left.

Instantly Tony sprang into high gear. As he did so, Rick cut his own speed and the Falcon beside him shot past then tried to keep himself between his Midwestern opponent and the goal.

The Falcon goalie's frantic shout to his defense came too late. The ball drilled by a panting fullback to curve inches away from the goalkeeper's clutching fingers. It struck the net with a solid, plunking sound.

Immediately the whole Midwestern squad converged upon Tony while the disgruntled Falcons stared at each other in disgust.

The score was chalked up on the board: Midwestern 5, Northern State 4, and a minute later the official's whistle signaled the end of the game. Instantly the whooping, shouting crowd spilled out of the stand to engulf the players.

Johnny grinned tiredly as he saw Cardenas boosted up on a pair of brawny shoulders. Weaver, too was seized and thrust high above the crowd.

Suddenly Rick pointed at him. "Get him up here, too!" he shouted. "He doesn't get off that easily!"

Later as they walked to the dressing room, Johnny

saw Mac Henson talking to Kay Roberts and Dr. Apperson outside the door.

"What kind of a crazy play was that?" asked Henson as he threw an arm about his goalkeeper's shoulder. "For an ex-quarterback, you play a great game of soccer!"

The coach turned to Kay again. "Better begin polishing up your adjectives," he said. "You're going to be writing a lot about this guy when he's on the varsity next season!" Then he added, "By the way, did he tell you about our party next week?"

Kay stared at Johnny in surprise.

"No, I didn't coach," he said. "I was saving that until later."